FORBIDDEN FRUIT

PETER H. COLLINS

I dedicate this book to my late wife, Josephine Collins,
my children, Gary and Melissa,
and granddaughters, Jessica and Sophia.

ACKNOWLEDGMENTS

I would like to thank my son, Gary Collins, for his unqualified support, enthusiasm, and belief in my novel.

Also, Linda Martin, Lynda Blackston, Denise Piddlington, and Sue Matoff for their wonderful feedbacks.

TABLE OF CONTENTS

PART I:
MILAN 2006

CHAPTER 1

My eyes opened to darkness, apart from a glimmer of light above and ahead of me. At first, I had no idea where I was until I noticed a tube inserted in my arm and an oxygen mask over my nose.

I then realized the blanket was raised above my legs and that I must be in some hospital...but where? I strained my eyes in the dim light to look at the wall clock with its large, luminous hands showing up in the dark.

A quarter to four it appeared to be, and then, as I looked to my left, the door of the ward opened, and a figure came in and started to inspect each patient.

I counted quickly. There were six of us. The rest were asleep with tubes raised high from their arms toward the ceiling, unaware of something just about to begin that would change my whole life.

Then I saw her. I could only describe her as an angel, sent for me to heal my wounds and give me back my life again.

Soon, she was coming towards me. She was small to medium build, perhaps 5'4," with her dark hair pinned up behind her and her blue uniform fixed neatly around her, taken in at the waist by a broad white belt.

It was her face that I could not stop looking at. Her large brown eyes, perfectly straight nose, beautifully shaped mouth, and a small dimple in the centre of her chin.

Then, at my next breath, there she was, standing right beside me.

She was a cross between Elizabeth Taylor and Jean Simmons, actresses whom I knew from old movies that I'd seen on T.V. Actresses that had struck me—not only for their acting ability but for their outstanding beauty.

"Hello," she said, "I'm pleased after all this time, you're back with us."

"Where am I, what's happened, and more important, how long have I been here?"

"You are in the St. Paulo Hospital just outside Milano, Italy. You were badly wounded in Baghdad from a sniper's bullet. The vehicle that you were in overturned, and you badly damaged your leg. You were found unconscious and have been in a coma for five weeks. You were flown here as we had the best facilities for saving your life."

I lay there quite shocked. I needed some more oxygen.

"What's your name?" I inquired, expecting her to say Elizabeth or Jean.

"I am Sister Maria, and I am here to look after you and attend to your every need."

My thoughts drifted to Julie Andrews, who played Sister Maria in the movie *The Sound of Music*, but this Maria had the face of an angel, and if she intended to get me better, I was all for it!

I thought of Maria from the movie *West Side Story*, played by Natalie Wood. The song went, '*The most beautiful sound I have ever heard.....*'

"Oh," I said. "Sorry, my thoughts were on something else for a moment; please say that again?"

Her soft, tender voice repeated, "I shall look after you and attend to your every need."

She held my hand and took my pulse. She then wrote the result on a clipboard attached to my bed, and I'm sure my pulse at that second was beating quicker than normal.

"Are you Italian?" I asked, noting a slight accent in her voice.

"Yes, but I spent many years in America, training to be a nurse, and some of my family live in New York."

That meant a lot to me, but I was still drowsy, and Maria told me to try and go back to sleep and that the doctor would see me at nine when he would do his rounds.

She smiled, and I realized she was still holding my hand. She then made her way to the other patients who were sleeping and eventually left the ward.

I closed my eyes and tried to go off to sleep, now pleased that I was alive, and I hoped that my memory would soon be back.

CHAPTER 2

In the Grand Hotel, fifteen minutes away from the St. Paulo Hospital, David and Sandy Gold had just woken up.

It was just after eight when their telephone rang, and Sandy, being nearest to the telephone in their hotel suite, picked it up.

"Hi, Mrs. Gold speaking."

"This is Doctor Rossi from the St. Paulo Hospital. I have wonderful news for you! Your son has regained consciousness!"

"David, Jeff's awake!" Sandy called to her husband, who was in the bathroom. "Sorry, doctor, I can't believe it. When can we come and see him?"

"Signora Gold, please could you come to my office at ten o'clock so I can give you the details, but I can say that the worst is now over."

David was now out of the bathroom. He grabbed Sandy as she put the phone down and hugged her. They had been in Milan now, since Jeff had been in hospital. They had prayed at the Guastalla Synagogue every day since they'd arrived in Italy. Both being devout Jews, they always felt that prayer would help them through their ordeal, and Hebrew was the universal language of every synagogue in every country that they happened to be in.

Back home in Laguna Beach, California, they lived in a three-story beach house overlooking the Pacific.

David was a successful lawyer and was head of one of the largest law firms in the States, with branches in Los Angeles, San Fransisco, Chicago, New York, and Philadelphia.

David Gold and Sons Inc. was the name of the consortium, and two of his sons, Gary and Michael, were senior partners.

On the American stock exchange, it had been quoted at $4 million, and only recently, they had put in an offer to take over the biggest practice in Miami.

Jeff was their youngest son. After graduating in 1990 in Political Science at the age of nineteen at UCLA, he was the rebel of the family. Only interested in the movies, football, baseball, and surfing, he was the 'All-American Boy.'

On his weekends, if the sea was fine, he took out his specially designed surfboard and spent hours skimming the waves near his own home on the beach.

He was strong and athletic, with broad shoulders. On top of his six-foot frame was black curly hair, large eyebrows, and piercing eyes that made all the girls just fall over to get to him!

Many a time David had suggested that Jeff study law, but Jeff just wasn't interested. Not that he was idle; he had taken a job as a part-time landscape gardener working around the Bel Air district of Hollywood, hoping that one day, a film producer might stop and ask him if he wanted to be an actor in some blockbuster movie.

He wasn't the youngest of the family. He had a sister called Lana, who was a couple of years younger than him and was studying to be a doctor.

When it came to religion, he rebelled. Although all his family were orthodox Jews and went regularly to the local temple, Jeff only went on the High Holy Days.

After he had lost his close friend, aged just seventeen, with an unusual heart problem, he could not believe there was someone up there. But he respected his family's beliefs, and every Friday night, he attended the family gathering to celebrate the Sabbath.

Round a large rosewood table, there sat David, his wife, Sandy, next to her Lana, and on the other side of David sat Jeff. The other sons, though, lived on the way to San Fransico and, being a fair distance away, only came with their families on special occasions.

It was a ritual: chopped liver to start, followed by chicken soup 'alla Sandy,' then chicken, roast potatoes, and vegetables. They always finished with homemade fruit salad as cholesterol was usually the topic of conversation, amongst others.

Then, one day, Jeff came home and told his family he had joined the army, and the shock nearly gave David a heart attack.

Jeff had wanted to do something good for his country, and since some of his friends from the surfing club had already joined up, he decided to join, too.

David was gutted. Sandy didn't stop crying, but his brothers and sister had promised to support him as much as they could.

After spending two years at the Military Academy in Washington, D.C., he found himself at the top of the class. Being a first-class athlete was not only an advantage, he also won the shooting and combat competitions.

Shortly after, he was posted to the Middle East, where he spent most of his army career. He became involved with the Iraq War and the Palestinian problems and learned how to speak Arabic and Hebrew.

It was a long time since he had seen his family, but fortunately, emails were reasonably frequent between the Middle East and California whenever it was possible.

He had been promoted through the ranks and was now a lieutenant with his own small battalion, and after helping to topple Saddam Hussein, an ambush in Baghdad, Jeff had been fighting for his life, and his army career was over.

CHAPTER 3

"Mr. and Mrs. Gold," Doctor Rossi started, "I have examined your son, who has made a fairly good recovery. In five weeks, we have fixed his leg, and all his other lacerations have healed nicely. I am pleased that although Jeff was in a coma, the situation helped his body mend more quickly. Doctor Di Carlo, the neurologist, said the brain scan had shown no damage, and as you know, Jeff is an extremely fit person. We will take him off the drip, and we will give him a diet that will help him build up his strength again. Also, he will have extensive physiotherapy by our top team on his left leg so that he will be able to walk again soon."

"Doctor, when will we be able to fly Jeff home?" Sandy inquired.

"I would really advise that he should spend at least a couple of months here, although I realize your facilities in California are as good, if not better, but we have brought him back to life, and the surroundings around here are beautiful. The gardens have never looked better, and it's peaceful. Jeff will get attention twenty-four hours a day from the finest staff in Italy."

Jeff's father, David, then said, "When you put it this way, you make it sound absolutely perfect, so we'll give you as long as it's needed. After that, he must be flown home. His recuperation can continue there, and in any case, I have an important meeting in Washington, D.C., and I really have to fly home."

"Very well then," said Doctor Rossi. "The treatment will commence tomorrow. You can see Jeff now if you wish."

With that, David and Sandy got up from where they were sitting, shook Doctor Rossi's hand, and made their way out of his office along the plush corridor to the left.

Jeff was situated at the other end of the hospital near the beautifully manicured gardens that contained tables, chairs, and umbrellas; it looked more like a hotel garden than a hospital.

David and Sandy had to admit that they had never seen anything so lovely. It was so peaceful there, and they were sure that they were making the right decision not to take Jeff home right away. David's law firm could take care of itself, and it was in the capable hands of Gary and Michael, plus the other senior staff.

Each day, David had spent time on the telephone at each of his offices, keeping up to date with everything. He was practically retired now. At the age of sixty-five, he only went into his Los Angeles office twice a week; the other days were spent playing tennis or golf or taking the new yacht that he'd recently purchased out. Thank God, he thought, that his health was still good, and after working so very hard throughout his life, he was now able to reap the rewards.

They finally got to Jeff's ward. The doors were open, and they could see him at the far end on the right, and there was the nurse with him they had met occasionally.

CHAPTER 4

"Would it be alright if I called you Maria?" I said to her, looking straight into her eyes.

She had just taken my pulse, which she assured me was quite normal, even though I believed that my heart just missed a beat each time she held my hand.

"Jeff, of course you can; if it improves your health, I will be glad to let you call me whatever you wish."

"Now that I am starting the physiotherapy tomorrow, will you come and sit with me when I am resting in your garden? Will you come in your own time and talk with me and tell me about yourself?"

"When I have finished my duties, I will try and find some time to see you, but you must realize that I have a family who lives in Stresa near the lakes. My mother lives there on her own as my father passed away last year. I try to go there when I can, but it's a good hour's journey, and I do not like to go there on my own. Sometimes, my brother, Lucio, calls for me and then brings me back, but this isn't always possible."

"I'm sorry," I replied. "I shouldn't have even suggested this, but you make me feel better every time I see you!"

At that moment, I saw two familiar people coming toward us. Maria turned, smiled, said good morning, and left without another word to me. I hoped that I hadn't said anything inappropriate. She seemed worried about something, and I felt a glow whenever she stood before me.

I then realized my parents were standing there.

My mother came to one side of the bed and bent down to hug me. "Oh, darling, how are you doing? We're so pleased you are back with us at last, and I'm glad to see those rosy cheeks appearing on your face again!"

"Mom, I feel much better, and I'm being looked after pretty good!"

My father stood on the other side of the bed, smiling. "How are you, son?" he said and kissed my cheek.

Coming from such a warm and affectionate family, kissing and hugging was quite normal, even in public places.

My parents were devoted to their family, and although we were okay financially, we were always taught not to be materialistic. So, we had to earn our bread and also appreciate that good health was more important than money.

Their marriage was one that was 'made in heaven.' They had grown up together, living in nearby streets in Brooklyn, New York. They had gone to the same schools together, and it was taken for granted that they would be married one day. So it happened, and the Silvers got together with the Golds. Everyone made a joke about their surnames, but after forty years of marriage, they were still blissfully happy, even though many of their friends had divorced and even re-married each other's partners.

My mother's family, the Silvers, were in the fashion business and had a large shop downtown. They were great friends with the Golds, who had a few bars in the city.

When my dad qualified as a lawyer, he spent three years with Alexander Joel, a small firm dealing in litigation. He worked his way to Senior Litigator before he heard that a large law firm in Los Angeles was looking for someone of his caliber.

Both his parents and Sandy's parents had been thinking for some time of moving West, as their health was on the decline, and one could guarantee good weather in Southern California. My father then applied for the vacancy, spending a weekend with my mother on the West Coast, and after getting the job, signed a contract that would earn him twice as much money as he was already receiving.

He gave in his notice and made arrangements to rent an apartment in Anaheim, not too far from his new office. Although Jeff's mother and father were not married yet, it was decided that both families would take the trek to new pastures. They managed to find condominiums in Laguna Hills and, lock, stock and barrel, moved out with furniture, which arrived after a few days.

Now, forty years later, both sets of my grandparents were in the Beth Shalom Cemetery, where there was a family plot.

My parents had four grandchildren, and I'm sure they were longing for the day they would be blessed with even more, as I was the one holding things up!

My father then said," You're going to be here for some time, and hopefully, soon, you'll be walking again; then you'll fly back to Los Angeles, and you could stay at our place for a while if you want."

I was lost for words, but kept thinking about Maria like nothing else mattered. I think that anything else that was said to me went in one ear and out of the other.

I knew Mom and Dad loved me, and I always thought I was Mom's favorite. Dad wasn't too happy about my career path, especially when I ended up in the army for fifteen years, and was probably wondering what I would do with my life now, as I could have a permanent limp, retire from the service with a pension, and a few medals to show off.

"Well, hon, we should go now. We've been here for two hours, and they'll be serving lunch. We'll be back later. Do you need anything?"

"No, thanks," I said, but deep down, all I needed was to see Maria.

CHAPTER 5

Time passed quickly. Lunch went on to dinner, staff came and went, and soon, it was time to go to sleep.

My parents spent a couple of hours with me during the evening, mainly talking about Lana, my sister, who had met a cardiologist who lived nearby, and things were pretty serious.

I was told that tomorrow, I would start physiotherapy, and I would be able to get out of bed and sit in one of those specialized chairs.

At one o'clock in the morning, I gave up trying to sleep. Any pain that I was feeling was from my head as my mind wandered from one thing to another about my past, present, and future.

How long would it be before I was walking again, how long would my recuperation be before I was able to start some work, and why was it that I wasn't looking forward to going home?

I had made many friends in the army. One was really close, and we shared practically everything. Samuel Casey had known me since the first day we enlisted. He came from a large Irish Catholic family and grew up in a small town called Barrington, just outside Chicago.

'Case,' as he was called by everyone, was like a brother to me and from training all those years ago to the present day, we shared one skirmish or another from Brooklyn to Baghdad.

He was not too tall but well built and weighed some one hundred and eighty pounds. He was very fit and could take care of himself if the situation arose.

But most of all, he had a talent for singing. Many a time, we'd be sitting in the officer's mess, and he'd sing like Frank Sinatra or Dean Martin.

Case came to see me the next evening, and apart from discussing how well I looked, the main topic was Maria.

"Case," I said, "I think I've fallen for a nurse."

"How long have you known her?" Case said in surprise.

"Less than three days, love at first sight, just like Tony and Maria in *West Side Story!*"

I then began to tell Case how it started, and as serious as I was, Case found it a little amusing.

"Have you said anything about your feelings? Don't you know things like this aren't supposed to happen with a patient and nurse, and what about her being Italian while you are American? She is obviously Catholic, and you are Jewish..."

"Jeff, it's an infatuation; don't even think of taking it further!" These words shook in my mind when Case left me.

Hours later, still unable to sleep, I looked at the clock on the wall, and it was now four o'clock. I rang the bell by the bed, and after a minute, the night nurse came. I asked her if I could have a small sedative to help me sleep. The next time I looked at the clock, it was four hours later.

The sun was already shining through the window, and the staff was busy getting the breakfasts ready. I was still tired, although I did manage to get a few hour's sleep, and when my breakfast was brought to me, all I ate was some cereal and black coffee.

Today, my physiotherapy was to begin, and hopefully, I would soon be back on my feet without the use of crutches, which I knew would be my support for the time being.

At ten o'clock, a young man came toward me, attired in a white jacket and trousers. He had a large smile on his face, and his dark hair fell neatly over his ears.

"Buongiorno, come sta?" he said. "Good morning; how are you?"

"I'm just fine, thanks for the Italian lesson," I replied.

"My name is Gino, and I'm here to give you some physiotherapy."

I noticed he had a wheelchair behind him.

Carefully, he lifted the bed covers with one arm around my back and maneuvered around so I could dangle my two legs over the side of the bed. Then a nurse came up, and between them, they moved me over onto the wheelchair, covered me over with a blanket, and led me to the elevator.

Five minutes later, we came to a room with large windows and a door that led out to the gardens. In the room, I could see the weights, a treadmill, a long table, and horizontal bars. It was like a mini gymnasium but with a hospital smell to it.

After being hoisted onto the long table, I rested my head on a pillow while Gino looked at my leg.

The scars had healed very well. Gino began to bend my leg up and down. Then, after a series of exercises, he spent the next ten minutes asking me questions and taking notes. "I don't want to do too much on your first day, but we'll meet tomorrow. But, as it's such a beautiful morning, how would you like to rest for a while in the garden?"

The idea of getting some fresh air sounded good, so after I had agreed to his suggestion, a nurse was called. Ten minutes later, I was sitting in the garden in my wheelchair under the shade of the cypress tree, reading an Italian/English phrase book that Gino had kindly lent me.

I was determined to learn some of the language, and I was a quick learner! I also wanted to impress a young Italian lady the next time I saw her.

26

CHAPTER 6

"Hi," a voice called to me.

I looked up from my phrase book, and there she was, looking down at me in her blue uniform and thick white belt.

Her beautiful eyes cast spells upon mine like I was being hypnotized at that very moment when she spoke to me.

"Hi, Maria," I said, trying not to feel excited at her presence. "What do I owe this pleasure?"

"I had some time on my hands and found out you were in the garden, so I came to spend an hour with you if you like?"

"Sono molto lieto!" I said, and she laughed out aloud.

"So, you speak Italian as well?" she said mockingly.

"I've decided to learn it so that I can say beautiful things to the most beautiful nurse that I've ever seen!" Well, I'd said it—got some of the feelings off my chest.

Struck from the shock of my impromptu reply, she looked for a chair to sit down on, saw one a few yards away, went to fetch it, and then sat down, trying to think what to say in Italian that I might understand.

"Tu sei molto sympatico, but then, if you want to speak Italian, you must say what you feel like an Italian does. As Italian is the most romantic language in the world, maybe I am only a little surprised by the way you spoke to me, even though it was mostly in English!"

We laughed together. I felt refreshed and not tired any longer. We talked about anything and everything. The beautiful lakes where her family lived, and then more seriously about how she nearly became a nun. As a novice, she realized that she would rather serve mankind in the medical profession than hide away in a convent in the hills, and anyway, she wanted to do something that *she* wanted, not what her mother wanted. Furthermore, her religion was always there, but she did not agree with a lot of the dogmas.

Other religions also interested her, and many a time, her feelings nearly got her into arguments with her family, whom she loved dearly.

I said that I felt the same way. It was my parents who were 'frum,' or religious, I explained, so it seemed we had quite a lot in common.

Before long, an orderly brought out some lunch of pasta and a cold glass of water.

"This is like a hotel," I said to Maria. "Mi piace molto!"

"Prego," she replied. "Don't mention it. We aim to please, and after all that you went through before you came here, you deserve it!"

Soon, it was time for her to go, and she said she would look out for me tomorrow around about the same time.

"Does that mean I won't see you on the ward?" I asked.

"Not for a few days," she said. "I'm on a three-day course." With that, Maria got up to go.

I raised my arm to shake her hand and say "Arrivederci."

She took it, held it for a few seconds as if she didn't want to leave, and finally said "Ciao, Jeff." She then turned and walked on her way through the doors.

I thought that life was worth living. Soon, as a nurse came to take away my lunch tray, I saw my parents coming toward me.

"Hi, honey," my mother called out, like I was still her little boy.

They came over to me, and both hugged me. While my mother sat down in the chair vacated by Maria, my father went searching for another to sit on.

It was hot now, possibly in the seventies. A porter came and put up the umbrella by our chairs to give us some shade, and it also stopped a light breeze that was blowing straight at us.

"How are you doing, son, and how did the physio go?" my mother asked me, along with a remark that every Jewish 'mom' would ask, "How are you eating? Got to get that strength back!"

They told me that Dad's brother, Abe, hadn't been too well, and they were both flying back home tomorrow as Dad had a crucial meeting at his Washington office on Friday in two days' time.

I was dying to tell them about Maria, but I was supposed to be a mature man, a lieutenant in the US Army, and this sort of conversation was only for buddies like Case.

"I'm pleased to see you've got a little color. This fresh air and good weather is just what the doctor ordered."

They spent the next half an hour discussing the family back home, and then an orderly came to take me back to the ward as the sky was getting a little

overcast.

They followed me to my bed, and then my father surprised me.

"I've made arrangements for you to stay a little longer here and convalesce until you are one hundred percent fit. Even though Southern California has everything going for it, this place is perfect for you, and I want you to have the best attention.

"I don't know what to say to you, Dad."

"Don't say anything; it wasn't too long ago, and we almost didn't think you'd survive, so don't thank me; thank the Almighty instead!"

He touched his small grey beard as he said it, and I realized that he really believed that all the prayers that he and my mother had said every day at the synagogue in Milan had something to do with my recovery.

How could I tell him that I was falling in love with a beautiful Italian Roman Catholic nurse at that?

"We're leaving tomorrow night for London," my mother said. "We just want to see my cousin, Irene, for the day before we fly back, so we'll see you tomorrow morning before we leave."

When I was back in bed, my parents hugged me and left, and, for a while, I just stared into space and wondered if me staying here longer and seeing Maria here longer was just meant to be.

As they say in most European languages, although it's probably spelled differently, '*Que sera sera!*'

CHAPTER 7

Three days passed. Each day, Gino came and took me for my daily 'exercises,' and he claimed I was doing fine.

The day that my parents came in the morning to say goodbye, my father told me he'd opened up a bank account for me in my name, and someone could visit me to help me fill out the usual forms and give a sample of my signature.

I was told there was enough money in there to tide me over for quite some time. Should I need any more, I only need to wire him for some money. But the days dragged, and although my recuperation was, in their words, *going to plan*, I sometimes felt depressed.

I sat in the garden for most of the days with my blue baseball cap keeping the sun out, and my Italian/English phrase book rested on my lap, but each word that I tried to learn wasn't sinking in, for my thoughts were of Maria.

It was Friday afternoon, and I asked if there was an English Bible handy that I could read. And no sooner had I asked than about ten minutes later, an elderly man in a black suit came through the door leading to the garden with a crucifix dangling from his neck.

He smiled at me as he approached me, and his eyes twinkled in the sun. With his short white hair brushed forward, he reminded me of the old actor Spencer Tracy.

"I'm Father Giancarlo," he said, stretching out his hand to me.

"Piacere," I said, "pleased to meet you!"

He sat next to me in a vacant chair and pulled it into the shade.

"So, Signor Jeff, you wish to read this Bible?" He held in his left hand a leather-bound book with gold leaf printing on it. I saw the words 'Holy Bible' in the middle and I was quite surprised that not only was I sent one so quickly, but the hospital chaplain had delivered it personally!

"Jeff. I hope that you don't mind me paying you a visit, as I was in my study nearby when your request arrived."

I admired his English. There was just a tinge of Italian accent. Otherwise, he could have passed as a Londoner.

"No, Father, I don't mind, but I don't think I'm up to having a conversation about religion or the Bible!"

"My son, if anyone asks for a Bible in this hospital, there must be a reason. I realize that you are Jewish by the 'Star of David' you wear around your neck. If you don't want to tell me, I will respect your wishes, but I am here for you if you are at all troubled."

I was amazed that he had noticed my small 'Mogen Dovid' around my neck, and his kind, soft voice made me want to take it further and speak with him.

"Father," I said, "I have been here some six weeks." I told him my story from the beginning. My whole life right up to the present.

He was a good listener and never once interrupted me. The only thing that I omitted was this feeling that I had, which was, to me, a 'forbidden fruit.'

"So now, Jeff, you have told me your life story. What troubles you that God has guided your path and given you hope of a new life? Why does your heart cry out when you should be thanking the Lord for all He has done?"

It was like I was in the confession box, though I can honestly say that I'd never been in one or near one, being Jewish. I had visited a few cathedrals in my time, but I now felt so close to the priest that I felt I could tell him anything.

"Father," I said slowly, thinking carefully of my words as I spoke. "I think I'm falling in love with a member of the staff here, and I thought if I read the Bible, I might find an answer somehow to my problems. I've never been that religious; my parents are, and their parents before them were, but me, although I am proud of being a Jew and even would have fought for Israel had the occasion arisen, I only celebrate at Passover time and the Jewish New Year."

"I'm sure, Jeff, that if you read the Bible, you will read lots of stories of how God tested His people's faith, no more so than the father of your great nation, Abraham, whom, as you know, was asked to sacrifice Isaac, his son. But this is taking it to the extreme, so read the book of Proverbs and read some of the Psalms of David, and maybe you'll find some answers.

"I have to go now, but if you like, I will see you here tomorrow."

"I'd like that," I said, smiling, and realized it was my first smile in three days. I also realized that we had been talking for well over an hour, and I was feeling once more relaxed and free from any tension.

"Ci vediamo," he said, which I knew meant *'see you!'* As he rose from his seat and shook my hand, his chain dangled from his neck. He then turned and walked towards the entrance.

I looked at the Bible I was holding, and the Hebrew words started coming from my mouth, "Shema Yisroel Adonai Eloheinu Adonai Echod"—*Hear Oh, Israel, the Lord, our God, the Lord is One.*

I had heard these words, which are the beginning of a prayer recited twice a day, and learned them as a young man at Hebrew School. For some reason, they had stuck in my mind.

No matter what I believed in, I did have my faith in something.

CHAPTER 8

It was now Sunday, and after my breakfast, I was engrossed in the Bible, reading the Book of Proverbs, and was fascinated with some of them.

Some I'd heard of before, and some were new to me, but when I finished them, all I still could think of was Maria.

I could still smell the fragrant perfume that she wore and pictured her in her blue uniform and white belt. I wondered what she would look like out of it, with her black hair flowing down her back? Would I ever be lucky enough to see her this way?

Things went almost at a standstill apart from the usual routines. I heard the church bells nearby inviting people to the Sunday Mass. I imagined Father Giancarlo taking the service somewhere locally, plus another in the hospital chapel.

As I sat there, a couple of hours later, reading the Psalms of David in the flowered gardens of the hospital, Father Giancarlo came as he said he would.

We talked about our different religions: how, in many ways, they were similar, the different holy days and fasts, and how close-knit the families were. I even told him a joke or two about a priest and a rabbi, which he found amusing.

He could see I was still troubled about my problem, and all he said was, "If you pray hard enough, my son, God will surely answer you in some way."

He didn't stay as long as the previous day, but he said he'd be back tomorrow. As he put it, "Today is time for my people and their God!"

My physiotherapy was coming along slowly but surely. With the help of crutches, I could walk across the room very slowly. I was just building up the strength in my left leg which was first place in the pecking order, but I was told the treatment couldn't be rushed.

Before I went to sleep that night, I covered my head with my hand and silently said a prayer that I knew from my childhood. "Shema Yisroel…"

I said a silent prayer in English, thanking the Lord that I was still alive and for my recovery and the good health of my family. I prayed also that there was the same feeling in Maria's heart as there was in mine, but could two hearts ever become one? Were Maria and I really forbidden fruit?

The night nurse came over to see if I was okay.

"Jeff, is there anything you want before I put this light out?"

Nurse Francesca, whom I grew closer to each day, was fair and petite. Again, and surprisingly, she also spoke perfect English, but she, unlike Maria, had learned the language at school and moreover, had told me that she'd had a few English boyfriends.

"Yes," I said, "would you sit with me for five minutes?"

"No more than that, Jeff, as I have some reports to do."

"Francesca, when you went out with these English boys, did you ever wonder if you would get serious with any of them?"

"Oh no, Jeff, I was on vacation when I met them."

"Surely, with all the nightlife and romantic music, something could have happened?"

"Well, maybe... There was one boy, but the trouble was, he wasn't Catholic, so I didn't let it go any further than a holiday romance. What else could I do? What would my parents say? Though, I have never been religious, and I can't remember the last time I went to confession."

"Do you know Maria well?" I asked,

"Si, if we manage to get days off together, we usually go out. Our favorite place is near the coast. Sometimes, we take our boyfriends, then they will drive. When the weather is nice, we will relax, eat and drink a little vino, and listen to an old Jimmy Fontana CD, you know, 'molto romantica.'"

"Yes," I said. "I've heard of him. I remember in the 60s, 'Il Mondo'—it was a big hit."

Then it struck me that Maria must have a boyfriend.

"Does Maria have many boyfriends, or is there one in particular?"

Francesca wondered where this was leading but still offered an answer. "She has no one in particular. With her job and her family responsibilities, she has no time for a steady boyfriend."

I didn't know whether to be pleased or not, but I decided not to pursue the questioning.

Francesca got up to leave.

"Good night," I said. "Thanks for the talk!"

It was Monday afternoon, and I was sitting under the cypress tree in the garden.

"Bongiorno, come sta?" I looked up from my phrasebook to see Maria standing there.

"Bene, e lei?" I replied with a broad smile, so pleased to see her again. "How did the course go, and how was your weekend?"

I had just finished lunch but was feeling a little sorry for myself as my leg muscles were hurting a little. I was in some discomfort, too, and honestly expected to be walking better, even with a slight limp. But when I saw her, I suddenly felt better.

"It went very well," Maria said. "And my weekend was spent with my family by the lake. It's beautiful there; you should see it."

"Perhaps you could take me there?" I said, expecting a negative reply.

To my glee and amazement, she said, "Perhaps if I ask Dr. Rossi, it could be arranged. A day out would certainly do you a world of good, and you have been stuck here all this time."

Maria sat down next to me, and we didn't stop talking. It was like we had known each other a lifetime and the difference of our ages didn't mean anything. I being thirty-four, and she being, I would think, in her late twenties?

As the sun went behind a cloud that was slowly forming, she got up to go and said she would see me later as she was on night duty this week.

"Maria," I called. As she turned to face me, I was lost for words and said, "Oh, it's nothing. *Ci vediamo*—see you later."

I returned to my phrasebook. "I want to make love to you," I muttered. "*Voglio fare l'amore con te.*"

I couldn't get the words out of my head. What was I thinking? And then, from the entrance, Father Giancarlo appeared.

"Bongiorno, my son, *come sta?* What a beautiful day! It makes you feel so good to be alive. How are your problems now?"

"I read what you told me to read, the Psalms, the Proverbs, and many other stories, but still, my problem is still there. Tell me, Father, do you know Stresa where Maria's family lives?"

"It so happens that I know Maria's family quite well. Her father, whom she was very close to, passed away last year, and Maria visits home most weekends if she has the time off."

It was like the gods were definitely on my side. I wondered if Father Giancarlo thought it was a good thing for me to go there. How could Doctor Rossi and his medical team say no?

Through the door came a nurse carrying a tray of tea and biscuits for the two of us.

"Mi piace una tazza di te," I said—*I'd like a cup of tea.*

"Your Italian is improving every day, Jeff!" Father Giancarlo replied, chuckling to himself. "But you must practice your accent!"

CHAPTER 9

"Bongiorno, come sta?"

I looked up from my phrasebook to see Maria standing there.

"Bene, e lei?" I replied with a broad smile, so pleased to see her again.

It was Monday afternoon, and I was sitting under the cypress tree again in the garden.

I had just finished my lunch, the sun was shining, and it would be another warm day, and now Maria was here.

"Did you have a nice weekend?" I said.

"Yes, my weekend was spent with my family."

Maria sat down next to me and, once again, we talked about everything.

Eventually, as the sun went behind a cloud that was forming, Maria got up to go and said she would see me later.

I returned to my phrasebook. "I want to make love to you," I muttered, "Voglio fare l'amore con te," I repeated yet again, "Ti amo, I love you, ti amo, ti amo…

" I couldn't get the words out of my head, what was I thinking?

And then from the entrance Father Giancarlo appeared.

"Bongiorno my son, come sta? What lovely day again, how are your problems now?"

"I still find it difficult, Father."

I then tried to change the subject.

We started to talk about the lakes and where Maria lived.

"Sister Maria told me how beautiful it is there, and then I said how I'd love to go there. She then mentioned that it could be arranged."

"It's not something that the hospital does with its patients, but since your father donated a lot of money toward some needy causes here at St. Paulo—and you are right; some of the scenery will take your breath away—I'm sure a day trip could possibly be arranged. As I told you before, I know Maria's family very well. So, it's quite possible this might happen. It could be a blessing, so let's just wait and see."

Then, through the door, as usual, came a nurse carrying a tray of tea and cookies for the two of us.

A few hours later, I was back in the ward with my evening meal, which was just a light tuna salad.

All I could think of was a lake surrounded by mountains with a few sailing boats drifting by. Would this be just a dream, or would it be reality?

Just before nine o'clock, Maria appeared, pushing a trolley toward me with a phone on it.

"Ciao, Jeff, there is a long-distance call for you from California."

The wire was plugged into the wall by my bed, and I picked up the receiver.

"Hi," I said.

"Oh, darling, it's Mom. How are you doing, honey?"

"I'm coming along fine; how's Dad and the family?"

"Your Uncle Abe passed away last week, so Dad's been 'sitting shiva' since last Monday. He's doing okay, and there were so many friends who came to see us and who attended the funeral. Your brothers and sister send their love, but I'm not sure when we'll be able to fly to Europe to see you."

"Don't worry, Mom. I'm doing fine here, and I'm being looked after so well. I'll be a new man the next time you see me."

"I'll phone you in a couple of days, Jeff. We're all thinking of you. God Bless!" Then the phone clicked, and she was gone.

I put down the receiver and sat staring across the room.

Today, I had been moved to a private room on my own, and although I didn't mind sharing a ward with five other men, the privacy had its advantages.

Five minutes after I had put down the phone, Maria came in and took it away. She returned afterward and sat down for a moment.

"I've got some good news, Jeff. On Saturday, we are going to Stresa for the day! I've spoken to Doctor Rossi, and he thought it would be good for you. We will leave after breakfast and get there for lunch at my mother's home. My brothers will probably be there, too, then we will walk down to the lake later."

"It seems that you have it all worked out. Have you booked a table for dinner at a restaurant afterward as well?"

Maria seemed a little surprised by my remark. "Jeff, you can't run before you walk. Is that the right expression?"

"Yes, Maria. I'm sorry, whatever you want to do will be fine. Anyway, we have to be back before it is dark, so I will look forward to it, and thank you for arranging this for me."

Maria got up and said, *"Buona Notte*, Jeff. As you say in English—sweet dreams."

She switched off the light and left the room. I closed my eyes in deep thought about the following Saturday and slowly dozed off to sleep.

CHAPTER 10

It was early Friday evening, and I had just finished my evening meal.

Who should walk into my room other than Samuel Casey, my close friend, who was working for a construction company just down the Adriatic coast, building the latest 5-star hotel?

"Hi, Case, how're you doin, buddy?"

"Well, I've been working flat out. We've got to get the Palace Hotel ready for six months' time, and I've been working seven days a week. It's just as well my girlfriend puts up with me, but Gina knows that I'll treat her well when I get off. In fact, next week, we're going to Rimini for five days. The best hotel, the best food, the best sex, only for my Gina!"

Sam sat there; his blue checkered shirt, white shorts, and deep suntanned skin made him look like a film star.

"How's the leg coming along, Jeff?"

"Oh, fine, but it's taking a little longer than expected. Two hours a day is all I get at the moment as it's a gradual 'build-up.' I'm having small weights now, so by the time they've finished, I'll be able to run a marathon!"

"How's Maria? Still got a teenage crush?"

I know Case didn't mean any harm, but I was not happy with the way he said it.

"Case, it's not a crush. I've never felt like this before. When she walks into my room or comes to see me in the garden, my heart misses a beat. When she holds my hand to take my blood pressure, I swear my heart palpitates louder than I've ever heard it before. Soon, I'll probably have bells ringing in my ears! And tomorrow, she is taking me to meet her family in Stresa for the day, and I feel like a love-sick teenager on his first date!"

"I just hope you know what you're doing, Jeff. Getting involved with a young nurse who lives over six thousand miles from your home is one thing, but how would your parents feel about it knowing she is not Jewish, considering how religious they are?"

"Religion doesn't mean that much to me, you know that, and anyway, it's not as if we're going to get married. Gosh, aren't you being rather negative about the whole thing? Let's face it: I may have a lousy time tomorrow, have a disagreement with her family, and find out they're connected to the mafia!"

Case could see this was a discussion he wasn't going to win, so we changed the subject. We talked for another hour about our respective families in Laguna Beach and Chicago and how he missed his home. He had been in Italy for two years and had left the army before the Gulf War.

He'd met his girlfriend Gina while sunbathing on a beach. He fell over her as she was sunning her back. Not looking where he was going, he had tripped over her and landed almost on top of her with his towel in one hand and his book in the other.

The shock of this turned the topless young lady over, much to Case's embarrassment, and after five minutes of Case trying his best to apologize in his best Italian, he found out that most of the swear words she used were in English!

From that moment onward, they were inseparable and eventually rented an apartment just outside Milan, where his head office was stationed, and near the beauty parlor where Gina worked.

It had been 'love at first sight,' as Case told me, so what was he doing telling me to be careful with Maria when the same thing had happened to him?

Eventually, Case got up, gave me a hug, and left, wishing me luck for tomorrow.

Soon, it was time to be helped back to my room—crutches and all.

CHAPTER 11

I was having difficulty sleeping as I was anxious about today, so I woke up early. What would her family be like? Would it be an anticlimax?

I had a light breakfast of fruit juice, toast, and coffee and then looked for the few clothes that I could see in my closet. I had sent one of the staff out to buy me some more clothes, and it was good fortune that not only did he have my taste, but was my build, and what he bought fitted me perfectly.

I had a shower and put on a white t-shirt and pale blue pants. With the white shoes and my tan from sitting in the garden, I was pleased that I didn't look like a patient from the hospital anymore.

Then, just as I was finishing shaving, Maria entered my room—I nearly cut myself!

I was looking at her through the mirror.

She wore a cerise-colored open short-sleeved blouse and a white skirt that went down to just below her knees.

Her hair was combed into a ponytail with a white band holding it together, and for the first time, her hair flowed down her back instead of being done up to suit her nurse's uniform.

On her delicate feet, she wore a pair of white pumps, and I also realized how tanned she was.

We hired a cab, which was waiting for us outside. We were helped into the back, Maria, myself, and my walking stick that I had just started to use. Before long, we were hurtling through the hospital gates toward the autostrada, which was some ten minutes away.

It was nice to smell the fresh air of the countryside with tropical trees on either side of the road. Little houses with colorful flowers in gardens and fields stretched out to the blue horizon.

After a while, Maria told me that we'd be there in fifteen minutes. The journey on the autostrada had taken just about an hour. Now, as we started to descend a hill, I could see the beautiful azure lake near Stresa ahead of us.

Soon, the signpost directed us to our destination, and we slowed down to take a country lane, which finally led to a gate.

Over the gate, I could see a stone-built house that looked like a farmer's cottage, which, as quaint as it looked, must have been centuries old.

Maria got out of the cab, opened my door for me to get out, and carefully let me put some weight on her shoulders as I put both my feet on the cobbled stones of the road.

She thanked the driver and made arrangements for him to call for us later that evening at eight so that we'd be back at the hospital at a reasonable time. My Italian was coming along fine, and I managed to understand some of Maria's conversation with him.

I hoped that I would pick up even more phrases during my day there, and some of maybe an intimate nature, which would only happen if the two of us were alone together.

Then I saw the front door of the house open, and a whole procession of people came out led by a young man in a cap, t-shirt, and tan-colored pants.

"Maria!" he called as he rushed to open the gate for us.

"Angelo, *ciao*," Maria replied.

The gate was drawn back, and Angelo hugged his sister.

"This is Jeff," Maria said.

"*Piacere, come sta?*" he said to me as he shook my hand vehemently.

We followed him to where his mother, Signora Carlotta, was waiting with two other young men that I guessed were Maria's other brothers.

Maria hugged her mother and then introduced me.

I was greeted like a long-lost son and then was passed on to the two other men, who I was told were Lucio and Gianni. Behind them were two little girls whom I found out later were Lucio's children. They looked like younger versions of Maria with long black hair hanging behind them, and since they had swimming costumes on, I guessed they had been swimming.

We then entered a hallway that was painted white, with two beautiful vases filled with magnificent flowers just inside the entrance.

The inside was decorated with paintings of the lakes and was fixed to oak panels. There were doors leading off the hallway to the main reception room and kitchen, and to my right was a large wooden banister with large carpeted stairs ascending to the landing.

"*Avanti*," I was told, and we all went into a large front room with a long brown leather sofa and two armchairs to match.

At the end of the room, in the dining area, was a large round oak table with six chairs around it. There was a long sideboard with pictures on it and another large vase of flowers. To the left of the table on the wall was a crucifix above two miniature statues of the Holy Mother and another, I thought, of a pope.

I wondered if Maria had told her mother I was Jewish, and while I was there, I had no reason to volunteer this information on the chance that it might spoil an ideal day.

We all sat down, Maria making sure that she was beside me. My stick was left out in the hall, and I nestled my bad leg carefully next to my good one. Then, Lucio went to the kitchen and came back with the bottle of red wine I had brought with me, opened it, and poured it into the glasses for everyone.

I heard that Maria's family business produced wine, and they had vineyards outside. I was told that Carlotti's Wines had flourished for many years and were exported all over the world. I felt a little stupid bringing wine with me as a gift, but Maria insisted that if I wanted to take anything, a good red wine would do the trick.

"Your health!" they all cried, toasting in my honor as we all sipped the sweet nectar.

"*Molto grazie*," I said, and then the conversation began.

"Di dove siete?"

"California," I replied. "*Dove la spaggia?*" I enquired—*Where is the beach?*

Not to be caught out, I was answered in English, "The beach is ten minutes down the pathway from our garden. It is a manmade beach, as it looks onto the lake."

"Maybe if your leg is not too bad, Maria can take you after lunch," Signora Carlotti said.

"*Sei sicuro?*"—*are you sure?* I said.

"*Si,*" came the answer from around the room.

Maria said, "The pathway is not too steep to the beach, and the exercise will do you good. We could go when the sun is shining on the lake, and we would be in the shade. It's more comfortable."

We sat chatting for another half an hour before Signora Carlotti said the lunch would now be ready.

Maria got me to my feet, and we followed her family through the main room onto a delightful terrace with an extremely large table covered in an embroidered yellow lace tablecloth. The table was laid for eight, and there were plates of salads opposite each chair position, with a large tureen of pasta in the center.

Once again, we all sat down, and the warm, friendly conversation went on between our courses and further bottles of chianti.

It was wonderful, and I felt as if I had known these people all my life. The time just flew by. After somehow squeezing through gelati, the homemade ice cream, it was two-thirty when I put down my napkin.

"Alora, time to take a walk to the beach," Maria said. "Stay here for five minutes as I want to collect a few things, then we'll go."

Soon, Maria returned with a large beach bag that contained two towels, sun cream, and a couple of drinks. There was also a large baseball cap for me and a straw hat for her.

"Just in case we're in the sun," she said.

CHAPTER 12

We walked to the end of the terrace, where there was a gate and pathway that led down to the manmade beach.

I held Maria's arm, and at a slow pace, we strolled downward until we reached the sand. The water was some fifty feet from where we stood, and as Maria had predicted, the sun was now behind us, shining onto a turquoise lake with the sun's ray stretching out to the other side of the land.

Small houses were scattered around the lush greenery in the hills above the opposite bay, and there were a few yachts sailing by with their owners enjoying the warm weather basking on the decks.

We found a secluded spot in the shade, and Maria spread a large rug out to sit on and our towels were placed behind us by her bag.

"This is the life!" I said. "Do you come here often?"

"When I want to relax and not think about anything, Jeff. The sea is warm also, and I am a reasonable swimmer. The privacy here is important, too, as this part is part of our home, and if you look both ways, you can see a wall that separates our place from our neighbors."

How convenient, I thought to myself and lay back, resting my head on the towel I'd made into a pillow.

Maria did the same, and for a while, we just lay there, eyes closed, and saying nothing.

I opened my eyes and looked to my right. Maria was looking at me like I'd never seen before. Her hair was now loose behind her, some covering her shoulder as she tilted slightly to her left side.

"I'm sorry, Jeff," she said. "I didn't mean to stare at you like this."

I thought I saw a tear in her eye and leaned over to face her. She looked so beautiful. I could smell her perfume now, and certain things were happening to me that I couldn't stop.

As she was lying there, I couldn't help noticing her pert and ample breasts showing through her cerise blouse that had opened at the top, and I tried not to look, as hard as it was.

"*Cosa c'e*, Jeff?" Maria asked—*What's the matter?*

"I could ask YOU that. Why are you trying not to cry? Why do I want to take your hand? Why do I want to put my arms around you and hold you tight? Why do I want to kiss you, and why have I never felt like this before? *Sei cosi bella*; you're so beautiful."

Maria looked at me, searching for an answer. She sat up and crossed her legs, holding them with her hands.

Oh, how I wanted to reach out to her, but I knew it could be fatal.

"Jeff," she suddenly said. "You and I are from two different worlds. You are from a rich Californian family, and I am from a modest Italian family here in Stresa. To make matters even more complicated, you are a Jew, and I am Catholic. Moreover, I have never been involved with a patient and promised myself it would never happen, so what are we going to do?"

"*Mi dispiace*, Maria"—*I am sorry*. "From the first moment I saw you, it was as though you were like a magnet, drawing me to you—an angel from above!"

"This cannot continue. You must realize this, Jeff," she said.

With that, I somehow got up and walked carefully down to the water, thinking of my next move. I looked out to the lake, and then, a few minutes later, I felt a hand on my back.

I turned and faced Maria. My right hand rose and stroked her flowing jet-black hair, then down the side of her cheek to her neck. I then put my arms around her tiny waist. I could not stand it any longer and drew her tightly into me, my lips touching hers.

The response was all that I had hoped for as her mouth opened, and I kissed her like I'd never kissed anyone before. I kissed her cheek and then her neck while my hands came from around her back to the front as I cupped her breasts in my eager hands.

"*Ti amo!*" I said—*I love you.*

We went back to where we were sitting, and we lay down on the thick rug in the shade.

It was sheltered by the trees, and no one could see us, I thought, but as I started to undo the buttons of her blouse, she grabbed my hand.

"No no, it's no good; I can't do this, Jeff, please understand!"

I stopped myself somehow with all the will power I could muster.

"We'd better go back now as we could sit by the pool," she said.

In one quick movement, she got up, dusted herself down, and then helped me to my feet. We then put everything back in the bag and walked slowly back to the house. Instead of us being close together, she just let me hold her arm without saying a word.

CHAPTER 13

At nine that night, I was back in my hospital room, resting in an armchair. It was dark outside, and I sat there reflecting on the day's events.

When we arrived back from the beach, we sat around the small pool for an hour, with everyone enjoying the sun, watching the two young girls swimming in the small pool, and talking quite naturally about our families.

Considering what had happened earlier, Maria was back to her usual self, talking in English to her brothers so that I would understand and to her mother in Italian, who only spoke a few words in English.

They were all so warm and friendly, and I felt like one of them. However, soon, it turned eight—the time when our driver was due to collect us.

We had eaten a tasty meal with freshly baked Italian bread with cheese, followed by fresh fruit. I don't think I had eaten so well in ages, but now it was going to be hospital meals again.

Finally, the driver arrived. I got up and hugged Maria's family. I kissed Signora Carlotti on both cheeks, walked out of the front door with Maria, and got into the car.

"I hope you will come back soon!" Maria's mother called out in her best broken English.

Then, off we drove.

"That was a wonderful day, Maria. Thank you for bringing me to your beautiful home and letting me meet your delightful family. As your mother said, we must do it again!"

"*Forse*,"—*maybe*, Maria replied. My hand moved slowly towards hers as we sat in the back of the car, and to my surprise, after everything, she let me hold it.

"Signor, Jeff," called out a nurse who had just come into my new private room. "There is a phone call from America; please pick up your phone."

"Hi, Mom!" I called out. "How are you doin?"

"Very well, Son, and what about you?"

"Oh, I'm coming along just fine. How's Dad and the rest of the family?"

"Just back to normal now. I bumped into Ruthie, your old girlfriend; she sends her love. She's still single, you know, she never got over the terrible divorce. I don't know why you two split up. You seemed made for each other."

The conversation went on for some twenty minutes, mainly about Ruth. Then, finally, my dad came on the phone and made up for lost time.

"Son, we wish we could fly out to see you, but the acquisition of our new office is taking time, and it will be at least another month before we can come to Italy."

"That's okay, Pop," I said, almost with relief. Maybe at this time, it wouldn't be a good idea to see them, as I wouldn't have to explain anything about Maria or tell any untruths. In another month, though, who knows what might happen.

Eventually, I said goodbye and put down the receiver. As I sat there, a large yawn came out of my mouth.

I got undressed, showered, and got into bed. By now, it was ten o'clock. My mind wandered to what my mother had said about Ruth, whom I had been dating for years before I left for the army.

There was definitely something between us, but I had felt too young to settle down. We liked and laughed at the same things. She was slender in build, had long blonde hair, bleached by the Californian sun, and jogged six miles every morning along the Pacific coast. She was also a good swimmer, and, all in all, we were great together.

I remember the night we made love for the first time in a deserted sand dune just as the sun was setting. The thrill of it as we ripped each other's swimsuits off, hoping that no one would walk by and catch us in the middle of an amazing simultaneous orgasm that would beat by far Meg Ryan's in the movie, 'When Harry Met Sally.'

It was something that I always treasured. If I ever made love to Maria, I wondered, would it ever come close? *It's all in the hands of the Almighty*, I thought. The trouble was that her God and my God were but one, but our religions were but two!

Gradually, my eyes closed, and I went off into a deep sleep. I woke up later and tossed and turned for the rest of the night. In my dreams, first of all, I saw Ruth the way she looked in her youth, and then Maria in her open buttoned cerise blouse just a few inches from my face.

CHAPTER 14

A month went by, and in that time, my physiotherapy increased, my leg grew stronger, and I was able to walk at a better pace. I must have walked at least a couple of miles a day around the hospital grounds, which were quite vast.

The weather now was in the eighties, being mid-July, and I could have passed for an Italian. With the help of an audio cassette tape, the language was improving quickly, but I was unable to use it on Maria as she had gone to visit her cousin in Sicily and had been away for almost three weeks.

I hope there's no Mafia in the family, I thought! Our relationship since the fateful day in Stresa had gone off the boil. Not that it had started, but from seeing me every day, Maria's visits were purely medical, and I realized that she had made up her mind. As the song goes, '*Our love could never be.....*'

My parents paid me a visit and spent a week here. Sometimes, we went out during the evening to eat. One night, we went to the Metropolitan Opera House to see '*Turandot*,' but the late evenings were tiring me out.

I first decided I was going to tell them about Maria, but then, as everything had died down, what was the point?

They then said their farewells and flew out to London, where my father had some business before returning home to sunny California.

It was a Friday afternoon, and after having a good workout before a hearty lunch of pasta, I sat in the shade in the garden, engrossed in the Italian/English phrasebook.

Suddenly, I looked up and saw Father Giancarlo walking towards me.

"*Bongiorno, come sta?*" I asked.

"*Ciao*, Jeff. *Bene, grazie*," he replied. He shook my hand, pulled up a chair beside me, and sat down. "You are looking very well, Jeff. According to the doctors, you should be well enough to fly home by the end of next week!"

"Oh," I said, a little disappointed, as this had been like my home for quite a few months, and it hit me that I might never see Maria again. Doctor Rossi had mentioned this to me, but it must have slipped my mind.

"Jeff," Father Giancarlo said seriously, "I've got some news for you. Had it been anyone else, I would not have said anything, but you are very special to Maria, and she wanted me to tell you."

I then felt a sudden shudder as if something was seriously wrong. "What happened, Father? Please tell me, please, everything!"

"Well, my son, Maria's mother has had a stroke, and now she needs full-time attention. Maria, being the only daughter, has decided to leave her position here and spend all her time with her mother. She will not be coming back!"

The shock hit me, and I sat up, holding onto the chair with both my arms. "I must go and visit Maria and her family," I said. "I must! I must!"

"I do not think it would be a good idea, Jeff, as it is a very distressing time for her family. She told me to tell you that she will contact you soon."

"But, Father, I am due to return to California in two weeks."

"You seem a very troubled person, do you want to talk?"

"Oh," I sighed deeply, and settled down in my chair. For the next half an hour, before the lunch was served, I told Father Giancarlo what had happened between Maria and me and the problems that we faced.

"My son, we are all God's children, and our paths are written before us. If Maria DOES feel the same as you, then you have to decide what is more important to you—love for each other or your family and religion. I know for a fact that although the Carlotti family are churchgoers and are at Mass often, this does not apply to Maria. She works very hard with long hours and has admitted to me that after all the tragedies she has seen at the hospital, her faith in Our Lord is not as strong as it should be."

"Father, I believe in fate. I was meant to be in this beautiful hospital and meet Maria. It was a miracle I survived the war, as most of my men never returned to camp that day. The fact that I am Jewish, and moreover, that my parents are religious and also worship every other day like Maria's, has nothing to do with it."

"If Maria wishes to see you, she will. She knows that you will return to California in two weeks and should she miss you, I am sure she will find your address and telephone number. Just be well, my son. Just say your prayers, and maybe the Lord will hear them." Father Giancarlo held my hands with his.

"Bless you, Jeff," he said, and with that, he got up to leave.

CHAPTER 15

In Stresa, the sun shone over the hills down onto the home where the Carlotti family lived.

Maria had just tucked a blanket around her mother as she sat in a shaded part of the terrace.

They sat together, with Signora Carlotti dozing off to sleep while Maria sat in thought, pondering where her life was taking her. Her brothers were at work and would return later with their wives.

Tests had shown that her mother had had a small stroke that had paralyzed her slightly, so she couldn't use her left hand properly.

She was told that, hopefully, with the right treatment, the paralysis would go away, but it wouldn't be rushed, and it would mean a visit to the hospital in Milan on a weekly basis. But since now Maria had a car, she could take her mother there.

Her thoughts then changed to Jeff and she realized how much she missed him. How much she missed their talks and walks, and then she thought about their moment by the lake and what could have happened if she had shown no restraint.

She wondered what it would have been like to feel his hands intimately touching every crevice of her well-formed body. To feel his hands between her legs and to succumb to him eventually and make love under the shade of the palm trees. *What could have been?* she thought.

At that moment, her mother looked up, "*Cosa c'e,* Maria?"

"*Niente,* Mama," Maria replied, but a tear appeared in Maria's eye, and she proceeded to tell her mother what she was thinking.

When she stopped, her mother hugged Maria. "*Capisco, cara,* Maria," she said, but she couldn't give Maria the answer she wanted. "It's in God's hands," she said in Italian.

The sun eventually went down toward the horizon. The few boats that had been sailing by disappeared from view, and the breeze from the passing wind grew stronger.

Angelo, Lucio, and Gianni appeared, bent down in turn, and hugged their sister and mother. Then they helped her up carefully and took her inside, for darkness would be descending on them soon.

That night, Maria couldn't sleep again. She took from her bedside drawer a picture that was taken of Jeff and her on the hospital grounds before his visit to her family.

They were so happy. Surely, she must see him. She would phone him!

She finally drifted off into a deep sleep but woke early the following morning as the sun was shining through the spaces of the wooden shutters over the window, casting thin lines against the wall behind the bed.

She could hear the birds singing happily, welcoming another pleasant summer's day, and she wondered what was she going to say to Jeff.

Then, just after breakfast, it was decided for her, as Doctor Rossi called from the hospital to say he would visit her and her mother at 2 p.m. that afternoon.

Not only was he the most senior doctor at the hospital but an old friend of Maria's parents, and usually once every couple of months, he would call and pay his respects. But this time, he also suggested that he would bring Jeff, as Jeff had been a little depressed lately, and a visit to the lakes would be good for him.

Well, Maria thought, *have my prayers been answered after all?*

CHAPTER 16

I was eating my breakfast when Doctor Rossi came in. "*Buongiorno*, Jeff, *come sta?*"

"*Bene*," I replied. "*E lei?*"

"Jeff, how would you like to come with me to visit the Carlotti's in Stresa? I must see how Maria's mother is, and I have some pills for her to take."

I looked at him with great joy and belief that perhaps there was someone up there looking down on me.

"We will leave at one, so have an early lunch. I will meet you in the reception."

After a light breakfast, I went to the physio department, where I did my usual exercises with my leg and spent half an hour on the treadmill. My leg was stronger now than it had ever been. My scars from my wound had healed nicely, and I was ready to return home to see my family in Laguna Beach.

A shower, a change of clothes, a shave, and a light lunch in the staff canteen, and I was ready to meet Doctor Rossi.

All the staff knew me, and considering the amount of money my father's foundation had donated to the place, they were quite happy for me to use their restaurant.

Soon, we were on the road, and just after an hour, we arrived at the family gate of the Carlotti abode.

It was very hot now, possibly in the high eighties. Doctor Rossi pushed the stone bell that was fixed just inside the right wall, and the front door opened.

There she stood, her raven hair again down her shoulders, two large jade-colored rings dangling down each side from her ears, with the same colored T-shirt above a loose 'seersucker' calf-length white skirt.

Her rose-colored lips shone in the sun, but tinted sunglasses hid her large, beautiful brown eyes.

"*Come state?*" she said to us as she came toward the gate, opened it, and let us both kiss her on each side of her tanned cheeks.

We walked back with her toward the front door and entered her home.

It was like I'd never been away from it. The fresh smell of flowers and the decorated walls with paintings everywhere.

"*Avanti, avanti,*" a voice called, "*qui,* here."

We walked through the main room and onto the terrace, where Signora Carlotti was sitting in her favorite chair.

Doctor Rossi kissed Maria's mother on each cheek. The doctor pulled up a chair while I was beckoned to the sunnier side of the terrace by Maria, which prompted me to put my 'shades' on.

"How are you, Jeff? How's your leg?"

"Almost as good as new," I answered. "My limp has practically gone; how are you doing, Maria?"

"I'm well, even better seeing you again."

I was surprised by her frankness and smiled at her, and then I stretched out my hand to hers.

She took it without any fuss, and said, "How would you like to walk down to the beach?"

I somehow came out with, "It was so good there, so peaceful, and there is so much I want to tell you."

"*Un momento*," Maria replied softly and went over to her mother and Doctor Rossi, who were deep in conversation, sipping a Campari each.

Then she returned with a smile on her face. "Jeff, I will go and get a bag with some food and a rug, and we will have a few hours to ourselves."

As we neared the beach, I could sense the excitement by the way we held hands on the way down the pathway.

Once again, there was no one to be seen, and the sun was still shining from the side of us rather than behind us.

I put the bag down, took out the contents, and spread the rug over the sand. Maria then raised her arms and took her jade-colored T-shirt off, revealing a white bikini top to match her skirt. At the same time, I stripped down to my shorts.

"Can you put some suntan cream on me, Jeff, before we talk? I do not wish to get burnt."

Maria passed me the lotion and lay on her stomach while I got down on my knees to massage her legs, which were already golden brown.

I started with her legs, her thighs, and then on her back. Then, her arms and shoulders, and as hard as I tried not to think about it, I felt my shorts become decidedly tight.

Maria then sat up and told me to lie on my stomach and started to put the lotion on me, and, as she worked her way up my legs slowly, it was really difficult to control myself, especially as she reached the top, inside my thighs. It was just as well I'd put a pair of briefs underneath my shorts.

By the time she had got to my neck, things had subsided a little, but when she was finished, we just lay there, and my feelings were so strong again that it took the utmost willpower to resist any temptation that might have been disastrous, at least that's what I thought.

We lay there for five minutes or so. I could feel the hot rays of the sun beating down on my back and legs.

Maria then turned over on her side to face me like the time before. She stared at me and squinted in the sun. "Jeff, you are going back to America very soon. Do you think we will ever see each other again?"

"Maria," I decided to choose my words carefully, "I have grown very fond of you these past few months, seeing you most days in the hospital, having you tend to my every need, always being there for me, and moreover, taking me to meet your wonderful family in such idyllic surroundings. Do you know how hard it has been for me not to feel something for you?"

"Jeff, I am a nurse; rather than go into the church as my parents wanted when I was young, I decided to serve my fellow human beings instead and have always made sure not to involve myself with patients for any reason at all. But with you, it was like you had this strong hold over me from the moment that you woke up in your hospital bed that night, not knowing where you were or why you were there. I was drawn toward you by a force that I couldn't control."

"It was like that for me, Maria," I told her, and at that moment, I drew her toward me with my left hand.

She did not resist. I pulled her head toward mine, and I raised myself to kiss her lips. Maria then moved over on top of me, the passion burning inside both of us.

My hands were now resting on the cheeks of her bottom, and I felt their curve. We were kissing passionately now, and my hands moved up from the base of her spine to her bikini strap that was holding her top on. I released the catch, the bikini slipped off her shoulders, and she moved her arms to let it fall to the rug. I took her breasts in my mouth one by one; I caressed them next as if they were the most beautiful things I had ever held.

Maria then got to her knees, undid the zip at the side of her white skirt, and pulled it down, revealing a white thong barely covering her pubic mound.

It was all done so beautifully. Nothing rushed. She slid my shorts off and then my underpants off and finally her thong, and we lay naked on the deserted beach, no one around, and no care in the whole wide world.

We touched and kissed each other intimately, and soon, I could not hold back any longer, and I entered her. It seemed like there was no tomorrow.

Never had I felt like this before. "*Ti amo*, Maria, *ti amo*," I cried out.

"I love you, too, Jeff," she said back.

And the next minute, we reached the height of wonder and exultation as we climaxed together.

We then separated and lay there, completely spent. It was a feeling that I had never experienced before, even with Ruth all those years ago, and I didn't want this to end.

We lay there with my arm around her neck. Nothing covering our intimate parts, just completely at ease. How could we not be together now?

CHAPTER 17

It was just after half past four. Doctor Rossi was pouring out a pot of tea for Signora Carlotti and himself when Jeff and Maria appeared.

"Ciao!" Doctor Rossi called out. "How are you? Did you have a nice time ?"

Maria and Jeff walked onto the terrace, holding hands tightly, trying not to make their feelings for each other too obvious.

Two more cups were put down on the table, and Maria poured out the tea for Jeff and herself. The two of them were in a dream world. Whatever Doctor Rossi or Maria's mother said went in one ear and out of the other.

The telephone rang from inside, and Maria got up to answer it. A minute later, she returned. "Doctor Rossi, it's the hospital for you," she said in Italian.

Doctor Rossi got up and went to where the telephone was in the hall. When he returned, he sighed and said it was time to leave.

The four people then went inside the house. Jeff and the doctor said their thanks for a lovely afternoon and then made their way to the front door.

Maria looked at Jeff with tears in her eyes. "When will I see you again? We have to talk."

"I have your cell phone number, and as soon as I can work something out, I'll call you." He bent down to kiss her goodbye on the cheek. He could feel tears running down her face. He whispered in her ear, "*Ti amo*, Maria."

"*Ti amo*," she replied.

They then made their way to the gate where the car was parked.

After what seemed like a longer journey, Doctor Rossi and Jeff were back at the hospital.

"Thank you so much for taking me, Doctor Rossi. You don't know how important it was for me."

The doctor looked at Jeff and smiled. "I know, Jeff, I could tell. The way you two looked at each other, I could tell."

Jeff made his way to his room, wondering just how could he return to his family six thousand miles away and forget the only thing that now mattered to him? But he knew deep down after all his parents had done for him, it would break their hearts if he did anything that was against their teachings and the way they had brought him up.

He sat in the armchair in his room and thought back to his childhood. His first school, his Barmitzvah at the Temple, the party afterward in Newport Beach, going to the Temple on the High Holy Days, and fasting on Yom Kippur, the holiest day of the Jewish calendar, known as The Day of Atonement.

And also at his cousin's wedding, when he promised his mother that not only would she stand with his father, under the Chuppah, the holy canopy where Jewish couples said their wedding vows, but with his new wife.

But now, it seemed like a betrayal if he were not to carry on the tradition that was expected of him and break his promise to her. So, he decided to write, as to see Maria would be unbearable, and he would not be able to go through with his decision.

The days started shooting by fast. Jeff was now at the peak of fitness, and he was due to go home in two days. His flight tickets had arrived, plus a car was arranged to take him to the airport.

Jeff felt so guilty, as he had tried a million times to pick up the phone and call Maria, and every time, he'd put the receiver down. The letter also that he was going to write was still not written.

He was sitting on the balcony of his room when he grabbed hold of the hospital writing paper for the umpteenth time. He then picked up his pen and started writing:

'My Darling Maria,

No words can express the feelings that I have for you, and please forgive me, my darling, for not telephoning you since our meeting. It was cruel of me, but I have thought very hard about our plight, and for once in my life, I prayed like I had meant it.

I know in my heart of hearts that our love could never be. We come from two different worlds, and our family upbringings mean so much to us.

It would break my parents' hearts if I didn't continue our strong religious traditions, and I'm sure your family would feel the same about you.

The Lord brought us together, and he has tested us. And if one day we should meet again, then we will know that our love holds no barriers.

From the moment I saw you, from the moment I kissed you, nothing else seemed to matter, but I am no longer in the army and will have to go home and find a civilian job. I can't afford to live my life as a 'beach bum' and whatever I have left of my life. I want to be a success and make my parents proud of me. They're not getting any younger.

Maria, please, please understand. Send my love to your dear family, and you know that one day, you will meet a young man and fall in love. Just remember the good times that we shared. You will always be in my heart,

Ti amo, Jeff.'

Jeff put down his pen and read the letter he had written. He read it again and again until tears came into his eyes.

At that moment, Father Giancarlo came into the room. "My son, *cosa c'e*? What's troubling you?"

For the next half an hour, Jeff told the priest of what happened and the letter Jeff had written.

"Jeff, you must see her; you cannot just send her a letter and leave. You owe her this much. You know, Maria will be here tomorrow with her mother at two o'clock, so why don't you see her then?"

Jeff hesitated to answer. "Very well, Father, but please can you arrange it? Ask her to come to my room before she leaves for home with her mother. I will be waiting."

Father Giancarlo left, and Jeff went to have a shower to clear his head before settling down for the night. Tomorrow was a big day.

He had to pack most of his belongings in his case, go shopping, and buy gifts for many of the staff who had looked after him and a special one for Maria.

It was his last day as he had a late afternoon flight from the Da Vinci Airport in Milan direct to Los Angeles, where his parents would meet him and take him down the coast to Laguna Beach. Then Jeff switched off the light and went to sleep.

CHAPTER 18

I woke up at six thirty. I had so much to do and such little time to do it.

After breakfast in my room of fruit juice, toast, and coffee, I asked if someone could get me a cab into Milan Centro to do some shopping. It was just as well now that I had a credit card as I needed the cash for the journey tomorrow.

At twelve noon, I was back in my room with plastic shopping bags from all the well-known stores Milan had to offer. I'd made a list out that numbered the twenty or so staff—from the head doctors to the kind orderlies—but my present to Maria was special. It was wrapped in a small red velvet-covered box and tied with a pink ribbon around it.

I intended to make my presentations as soon as I could, so after a quick pasta in the staff restaurant, I went on my journey throughout the hospital, which had become my home, handing out the many gifts and getting hugs and kisses and best wishes from each person.

It was two-thirty, and I knew Maria must have been there with her mother and that Father Giancarlo would have asked them to come and see me before they left.

I got back to my room and found Maria and her mother sitting in two seats outside my door.

They stood up, and I greeted them both.

"Signora Carlotti," I said, "I wanted to say goodbye to you as I have grown very fond of you and will miss you and your family very much."

As I thought it would happen, she looked at me while Maria translated all that I'd said, and then she put her arms around me and hugged me.

"*Un momento,*" I said and opened my door, returning a few minutes later with a cut glass vase I had bought.

I gave it to her.

"*Grazie, grazie!*" she said and hugged me yet again.

"*Voglio parlare con Maria, per favore da solo?*" I asked.

She understood, sat down, and Maria followed me onto my bedroom balcony.

We sat down on two chairs, and I took Maria's hand. I picked up the letter I had written to her and prayed that I would say the right words.

"Maria, I wrote this letter to you, but I could not leave without speaking to you in person. It was easier to write, but I feel that I must read what I have written, so please, just listen."

I began to read out my letter. "My Darling Maria," I began.

When I had finished it, Maria was crying. "*Capisco*," she said—*I understand.*

I then picked up from under my chair the small box wrapped with a pink ribbon on it.

"This is for you. I hope you always wear it in good health and as a reminder of what we meant to each other and to keep me in your heart."

Maria carefully opened the wrapper and box. Inside, nestled on a bed of red satin, was a solid gold 'Star of David' on a chain.

"It's only a small one, so it is not too noticeable, and if you wear it next to your cross, that will make you a 'Catholic Jew,'" I joked, but it didn't come across as a joke, and more tears now poured down Maria's face. I leaned forward to hold her and stood her up, holding her tight.

I then took the chain from the box, went behind Maria, and fixed the chain around her neck.

"It's alright now," she said after a minute, and I led her back into the room to rejoin her mother.

Signora Carlotti got up to go and held Maria's arm. They turned to me for the last time and said, "Vai con Dio! God bless you, Jeff!"

"*Arrivederci*," I replied and opened my door to let them out.

Then they turned and went out of my room without looking back.

PART 2:

CALIFORNIA

CHAPTER 1

The time finally arrived, and I said my very last goodbyes, gave out the remaining few gifts I still had on me, and left the hospital that had been my home.

After a thirteen-hour flight, I landed at 8 p.m. Los Angeles time.

It felt like six o'clock in the morning for me, but I did manage to get some sleep on the plane.

"Hi Jeff, how yah doin?" I heard as I came through the 'Arrivals.'

It was my oldest brother, Gary, not my parents, who was waiting for me.

I called him the 'shaved one,' as he was well known because he always shaved his head and looked a lot older than his forty-two years.

Always with a smile on his face, he did not look like your actual lawyer in his checked shirt and leather jacket, but when he was in court, you could have been listening to Perry Mason. Talk about verbal diarrhea—Gary just didn't stop talking!

Gary gave me a hug, grabbed hold of some of my baggage, and we made our way to where his car was parked.

As we drove down the Freeway to Laguna Beach, we did not stop talking. I spoke of my stay in the hospital and that I had met someone whom I'd fallen for in a big way, but due to certain circumstances, however, it hadn't worked out.

Knowing my brother, I didn't want to go into any details, as he wasn't one to keep quiet about things.

"How are the family?" I said. "And how is Melissa and the kids?"

"Oh, Melissa's fine, busy with her charities—on every committee you can think of!"

"And the kids?" I inquired.

"Well, Donna's studying law in Washington DC, and Bradley's at medical school in Philadelphia. Both are having a great time, I hear, but working hard.

They're great kids and come home to visit whenever they can."

Soon, we were driving down the highway that led to the Pacific Coast, and it was not long before we came to a 'T junction.'

There, ahead of me, was the blue sea, the beach, and the playground where I used to practice my basketball when I was young. To the right was Newport Beach, and to the left was Laguna Beach.

We turned left and made our way down the coast road. It was how I remembered it. A few shops and restaurants on either side, a few people leaving the beach for their homes, the sun slowly going down, and the evening traffic flowing past.

Five minutes later, we arrived at Beach Drive, where the family home was.

Gary now lived down the coast in Dana Point and had a beautiful four-bedroom home not too far from the harbor.

Michael, my other brother, lived up the coast in Seal Beach, while my sister, Lana, had recently moved into a rented apartment near him.

We stopped outside a white double doored white building with a garage on either side of the entrance.

As we got out of the car, Gary fetched my baggage from the trunk, and the two of us walked up to the front door.

Because of the security, there was no door key but coded numbers to press, just like the bank. It had always been like this, as the property had to be at least $10 million or more.

Gary pressed the six digits to enter, and the door opened into a white interior. To the left was an elevator to the lower floors, further on was Mom and Dad's bedroom next door to the gymnasium, and to the right was a spiral staircase with chrome banisters.

The house was on three stories. The first floor down was where I used to sleep; there were also two other bedrooms, and each one led to a terrace overlooking the Pacific Ocean.

On this level also was a room with a pool table, a lounge with comfortable furniture, and a large television screen that appeared from the ceiling at the touch of a switch.

On the lower or bottom floor was a massive kitchen and dining room area, which once again opened onto the terrace, and a living room and lounge suite that seated ten people comfortably around a table.

We arrived at the bottom floor and exited the elevator, most of my belongings I had left upstairs, and I could see my mom and dad relaxing on sun loungers, reading.

"Hi, Mom and Dad, how are you?"

They turned, stood up, and gave me a hug. "Jeff, we're fine; wow, you look marvelous. That place certainly did you a world of good!" my mother exclaimed.

"If you wish to stay here tonight, your room is waiting for you, just as you left it," my father said. "But come and sit down for five minutes and tell us about your health?"

"Thanks for the offer, but I want to get home. My health is fine, thank you."

Twenty minutes later, I was still talking. I really needed to unpack a few things and take a shower.

I made my excuses and decided to leave. I made my way upstairs to the room I had grown up using as a young child.

Gary had now gone, so I said goodbye to my mother, and my father followed me to the front door.

The door opened, and I loaded my things into my father's car, and he drove me to my home. I then hugged him, thanked him for the lift, and off he went.

Once inside my home, I unpacked, put items for washing in the laundry box, and went to take a shower.

The hot water, *thank goodness*, woke me up. I dried myself and returned to my room, opened the doors to the terrace, and walked out to look at the wonderful view across the bay.

Although it had been a lifetime since I had left home, it seemed as if time had stood still. It was peaceful, the blue sea was calm, and the beach was deserted.

Before I joined the army, I had bought this place, which was just up the highway from my parents. I cooked there for myself, but my mom's cooking was the best! As they say, Jewish chicken soup is 'penicillin' and a cure for everything.

Then I thought of the many times in the past when, growing up, I was able to talk to Mom about everything, but this was a little different.

I must have had Maria on my mind while I was there before because my mother had turned to me while my father was out of the room and said, "Jeff, you seem miles away; I know you're old enough to have a family of your own, but there's something on your mind, and if you want to talk to me about it, I'm willing to listen."

I thought for a moment. I didn't feel like a 'thirty-something' mature male. I was supposed to think about the future, go forward, and not think about the past.

"You couldn't help mom; no one can."

"Try me," she said. "Whatever you've done, I'm still your mother, and surely it can't be that bad?"

"Mom, when I was in hospital, I met someone who nursed me back to how I am now, gave me great strength and belief in myself, and was always there for me. We formed a wonderful relationship, and she even took me to meet her family, who lived by the lakes in Stresa."

My mother sat and listened without saying a word as I explained who Maria was and how we had fallen in love without going into intimate details.

I had said enough, and I finally stopped. My mother rested her hand on my knee and said, "Jeff, you are old enough to make up your own mind. We are a religious family, but whatever we do to keep the religion, we cannot expect our children and grandchildren to feel the same. It would break your father's heart if you didn't marry a Jewish girl even if you are not religious, but to marry a Catholic girl, I believe you might have to convert to her religion. Your children would be brought up as Catholics, so Jeff, my advice is to forget her. Time will heal your broken heart, and you will find someone else that you have more in common with and is Jewish."

It was what I expected my mother to say, and I knew deep in my heart that she was right.

I was now finding it hard to stay awake, and my eyes were gradually closing. It was nine o'clock LA time, so I thought I'd have an early night and go to bed.

CHAPTER 2

The moment my head had touched the pillow last night, I was dead to the world. I woke up at eight the next morning.

I got out of my bed and went to the bathroom and showered. Then I returned to my room, put on a short-sleeved shirt and shorts and made my way to the kitchen. The sun was shining into the room, the terrace doors were open, and a welcoming breeze of fresh air was coming in from the Pacific Ocean.

Then I put all my breakfast on a tray and walked out into the sunshine where not only did I find a table and a chair, but I saw Lana, my beautiful sister—who must have let herself in—fast asleep in a lounger, with a shade over her face.

I couldn't remember how long it was since I'd seen her, although we had written to each other while I was in the hospital, but it was years since we'd met in person.

Not to wake her up from her slumber, I quietly ate my breakfast of bran flakes, bagel, and coffee and then wandered over to the wall overlooking the cliff.

It was a splendid view. From the south along the coast to the north were miles of golden sand; above the cliffs were beach houses, many owned by famous pop stars, film stars, producers, and directors.

From Dana Point up the coast to Newport Beach and beyond, it had to be seen to be believed, and no one was bothered by landslides, forest fires, or even an earthquake that could strike at any time.

Suddenly, I felt a hand on my shoulder. As I turned around, two arms were put around my neck.

"Hi brother, how are you? I let myself in; I hope you don't mind. I've also been looking after your home for you while you have been away."

I gave Lana an almighty hug and kiss. "I'm okay. Thanks, sis, and you don't look too bad yourself; let me have a good look at you."

Lana stepped back and did a twirl. She was five-two, one hundred and ten pounds at a guess. With long blonde hair and her tan, she looked like a film star.

"Wow, you look great. My God, you don't look a day over twenty-five! What are you doing workwise, Dr. Gold?"

"I'm at the Tonkon Institute in Santa Ana, which is connected to Santa Ana General Hospital. Still looking for new ways in heart care. I do some lecturing also, which pays good bucks, but at the moment, I'm on a week's vacation.

"Still no man in your life?" I inquired.

"There is one, but he's married, soon to be divorced, and we've known each other for almost two years. Richard is also a doctor and lives in Villa Park. He's forty years old with two teenage children."

It didn't surprise me that Lana had volunteered all this information without me asking, as she was like an open book, and we had always been very close.

"I'm sure you know what you're doing. Have Mom and Dad met him?"

"Of course not! Besides the fact that he's forty, he's a very liberal conservative Jew who doesn't keep kosher, let alone most of the holidays! Can you imagine what Mom and Dad would say about that? The one thing going for him, though, is that he is so charming and handsome, he would definitely win our rabbi round!"

"I'd like to meet him; maybe the three of us could meet for a coffee one evening? He sounds just the kind of person I'd like to be close friends with!"

"I'm meeting him later tonight. Do you want to come with? We could meet at the Laguna Hotel at eight, maybe a meal after?"

"Fine," I replied, "I'll meet you there at seven-thirty."

With that, Lana kissed me on the cheek and sat down next to where I sat.

I sat down on the lounger, rubbed some sun cream onto my body, and turned to face the sun, pleased now that the long scar had practically disappeared. And with a decent tan, one would never notice it.

Twenty minutes went by, and then Lana got up from where we were both sitting, kissed me, and said goodbye, and that she'd see me later, just as my mind wandered back to Italy and Maria.

I was thinking of that day on the beach. That special day. I was playing it over and over again in my subconsciousness. I even called out, "Maria, *ti amo.*"

I felt embarrassed. What did Lana hear, and what did she think? How should I answer her?

"Oh, it was just some movie I saw while in Italy. One of those romantic ones," I said before Lana wondered what on earth I was talking about.

It seemed to do the trick, anyway, so I quickly changed the subject.

I decided to pop into my parents' later. When I arrived, my mother was just unpacking some shopping.

I asked her, "What did you buy at the Deli?"

I could see there was a large plastic bag just inside the kitchen entrance with some bread sticking out of the top.

"Oh, the usual: some lox, chopped liver, corned beef, and rye bread, which will be enough to last until tomorrow!"

"Jeff," my father then said, "have you thought about finding a job?"

I had no proper qualifications, and at my age and with only an army pension to live on, I needed to think about the rest of my life and career. Over the past few months, I never once thought about what I was going to do when fit. My thoughts were about getting well and enjoying my relationship with Maria, so what now?

It suddenly hit me. What was I good at? What could I do to earn a decent living? I had to be positive and realize that I would not rely on my parents' charity for much longer.

"Dad, tomorrow I shall do something about it; tomorrow is the first day of my new life!"

Then, the three of us went into their living room.

CHAPTER 3

The days and the weeks went by, and Jeff eventually found a job as an assistant soccer coach at UCLA. He had taken a course and had passed it with flying colors. After spending hours every morning in his parents' home gym on the top floor of their home, he was back to peak fitness.

Jeff's beach house was a few miles away, which his father had helped him buy as an investment a few years before Jeff left for the army.

It was literally right on the ocean. You could open up the patio doors, walk down some thirty steps, and you were on the beach.

It was peaceful there, but sometimes Jeff was lonely and spent most of his day, when not working, at his parents.'

He also studied videos and DVDs on soccer, learning all the latest techniques from the U.K., Spain, Italy, France, and South America.

When he was at school, he was captain of the soccer under 16's team, and although he excelled in most sports, he enjoyed soccer the best as it was a great team game, and gave him a great social life.

He had made good friends with one of the other coaches, whose name happened to be Nat Cole, and Nat had always been the subject of gags because of his famous name, although his father's original name had been Cohen.

Everybody asked Nat to sing them a song, but on hearing his voice, he quickly disappeared from view.

He was a tall, well-built guy in his thirties with fair wavy hair, which was long enough to wear in a ponytail. His close friends sometimes called him Natalie for a joke, but he took it in good spirits.

With a different girlfriend every other week, Nat was very popular with the opposite sex, and many times, he would try to get Jeff lined up on a double date.

Jeff, though, hadn't been interested at first, but one evening, when Nat was around at Jeff's house, a picture of Nat's latest flame taken at the Laguna Night Club made Jeff sit up and stare at the photo.

"Wow!" Jeff exclaimed. "And where on earth did you meet her?"

"Oh, she came to watch her brother, Ed, play basketball a couple of weeks ago. Every time Ed scored, Beverley jumped up and down so excitedly, I thought she was going to have an accident as the top she was wearing barely covered the top of her ample boobs!"

"I see what you mean. Does she have a friend?" Jeff asked.

"I can always find out; it's about time you started dating and finally got Maria out of your system!"

Jeff thought about Nat's last remark. It had been quite a few months since he left Italy, and although things had been easier with his new social life, he had hardly looked at a woman.

The few dinner parties he'd been to were with married friends, and if Jeff had been matched with anyone by the end of the evening, he just didn't want to take it any further.

"I know," said Nat, "on Saturday evening, Beverley has asked a few close friends round to her home in Newport Beach. Why don't you come over? There are always a few single ladies there, and some are really good-looking. Beverley won't mind. I've mentioned you to her many times, and she thinks of you as a war hero. I'll pick you up at eight. Wear casual and bring a pair of swim shorts with you as she has a pool."

Jeff thought it was a good idea as his social life needed improving, and he had been celibate far too long.

After Nat had gone, he phoned his parents to see how they were, had a shower, and then settled down to read the sports paper before going to bed.

CHAPTER 4

It was Saturday night. I got myself ready and felt very good at the thought of the evening ahead at Nat's girlfriend Beverley's home.

Right at eight o'clock, my doorbell sounded, and I eagerly went to open it.

There stood Nat in a pair of beige pants and a white short-sleeved shirt, and hair brushed into his usual ponytail. But he wasn't alone, as just behind him was a lovely lady who could have jumped out of the 'Playboy Magazine Centrefold'!

I stared at her rather too much, not taking my eyes off this tanned beauty wearing a white catsuit and little else, with a zip all down the front. Her nipples were showing through the outfit, and from what I could see, she had no knickers on either!

"Oh, this is Janine," Nat said. "Beverley asked me to pick her up on the way to you."

"Come in, please. I won't be a minute."

As Janine entered, she hugged me and pecked me on the cheek. "Great to meet you, Jeff. I've heard so much about you from Nat and Beverley: *a war hero!*"

She smiled at me, and it felt as if I was greeting my long-lost relative. It couldn't have been a better start.

I asked them to take a seat while I locked up all the windows and doors. Then I returned, and the three of us left to get into Nat's car, which was waiting outside.

The ride to Newport Beach was only thirty minutes away up the Pacific Highway, and as we sped past some magnificent homes, we suddenly came to one that looked like a Spanish-style 'hacienda.'

It was a single-story home painted in yellow with a large driveway and electronic gates at the entrance.

We stopped, and Nat got out to press the buzzer situated just inside the wall. After announcing who we were, the gates opened and we drove our car to where there were another four cars already parked. Then we got out and rang the front door.

It was Beverley who opened it as I recognized her from her photo, and *my gosh*, she was wearing a striking printed chiffon 'wraparound' dress, which looked as if it was done up around her waist with a bow that accentuated her marvelous figure.

"Hi there, come in and make yourselves at home," she greeted us with kisses on our cheeks.

The three of us entered a circular hallway with a floor in grey patterned marble, which led through to her main large reception room. This was fitted with leather sofas and chairs, large pictures on three walls, two pots of large tropical plants, and then patio doors that stretched some thirty feet and opened up to a floodlit swimming pool, as, by now, the darkness was almost upon us.

In the corner of the room was a large table with food and drink, and four other couples were helping themselves to a feast of pasta, chicken, salads, and the best Californian wines.

I wondered how Beverley came to be living in such a home, as it could have been a movie star's residence, but I guess I'd find out later.

Janine grabbed hold of my hand. "Come on, Jeff, let's get something to eat; I'm famished!"

We wandered over to where the food was, and as we passed the other guests, Janine introduced me to them. The men were probably in their thirties, and their partners looked much younger.

They all said they were happy to meet me, and Janine told them I was a *war hero*, much to my embarrassment.

We helped ourselves to some food and wandered outside to where there was a vacant bench, where we sat down to devour the pasta that I had and the chicken that Janine had.

"I don't know anything about you, Janine, so why don't you tell me where do you live and what do you do?"

"Well, Jeff, at the moment, I am appearing in a show at the President Hotel in Las Vegas. Tonight's my night off, so being a good friend of Beverley, I was invited here. The flight to Orange Airport only takes two hours. I come from San Diego originally but studied acting and dancing in New York at the Academy of Drama and

Dance. I've been in a few well-known musicals but would like to do more serious work. Because of my work, I keep fit every day, run two miles, and swim four lengths in the hotel pool. I also watch what I eat and go to the best beauty parlor on the 'Strip.'"

"I can certainly see that," I told her as I couldn't help glancing at her white catsuit, the zip at the front gradually slipping lower to show the outline of her breasts.

"Do you do any photography or modeling work?" I inquired.

"I used to. I was 'Miss July' in last year's 'Miss Las Vegas Magazine.'"

"That figures, and pardon the pun, but you're very attractive, and I feel flattered that you're the slightest bit interested in me!"

"Well, honey, I go for the dark-haired men, and I can see that you keep yourself fit as well!" She moved closer to me and whispered in my ear, "Your aftershave ain't that bad also!"

For the first time in ages, I felt stirring in my pants. Was this a 'come on,' or was she just flirting?

From an old line I had heard once, I said, "If I told you that you had a nice figure, would you hold it against me?"

She smiled and said, "Jeff honey, I've just got to go somewhere as I think maybe I've drunk too much wine, but I'll be back soon. Don't move from there."

I sat there looking around the amazing surroundings, and even though we were outside, it was still very warm, considering it was now gone nine, and the guests were already in the pool.

Some ten minutes later, Janine returned with what looked like a spliff in her hand.

She had taken our trays of food away when she left me, and when she came back, she took my hand and said, "Follow me, Jeff."

We got up and made our way down a narrow path, and five minutes later, we found a shaded spot that had a couple of enormous 'loungers.'

There was no one around. Janine was still holding my hand when we sat down, and she took a drag of her cigarette.

"Do you want to share it?"

"No thanks, I'm really not into that," I answered.

Then, after one large inhale, she threw the spliff to the ground, stubbed it out, and turned to face me, placing her hand on my thigh.

With the other, she reached for the zip of her catsuit and slowly pulled it down, exposing her well-formed breasts and letting them come out.

She then took my other hand she was holding and placed it on her left breast, leaned toward me, and kissed me on the side of my neck just below my ear lobe.

Soon, her hands were all over me, and I felt a bulge in my pants, which she noticed and decided to unfasten my zip.

Before long, we were stretched out on the lounger, almost naked, having the most amazing time. Trying things that I'd never experienced before.

Her flowing blonde hair fell over her ample breasts, and I just lay there while her body did the rest!

Her moaning, which started gradually, grew louder and louder until neither of us could hold back anymore....

CHAPTER 5

It was mid-day on Sunday morning. I had just woken up and had to pinch myself to check that it wasn't a dream last night.

***

I had arrived home at about two o'clock. I remembered Nat dropping Janine off first at a small hotel where she was staying for the night, and then he dropped me off.

I remembered that after making love with Janine, we somehow got up, put on our clothes, and walked around the garden to where there was a changing hut. Then Janine took out of a small purse she was carrying a bikini bottom, took the catsuit off again and put the bikini bottom on.

"Come on, Jeff, let's go for a swim in the pool!"

I once again took off my shirt, pants, and shoes, and after leaving our clothes in the hut, walked to the edge of the floodlit blue pool before diving into the heated water.

Soon, others joined us. No one seemed to care that the women were topless since one could see this all over the beaches along the coast.

We spent some thirty minutes in the water before getting out, drying off with towels provided, dressing, and going inside the house for a hot drink.

By now, it was gone ten, and people were dancing to a Rolling Stones CD. When that was over, the mood changed to a slow, smoochy Italian CD, which reminded me for the first time in ages of Milan and Maria.

One of the tunes played was '*I Can't Get You Out of My Heart*,' which was a very popular tune, and I started humming this as we danced.

"Oh, you must know these tunes from your time in Italy," Janine said as I held her tightly round the waist and rested my cheek against hers.

I agreed, but at the same time remembered the Elvis Presley number, '*She's Not You!*'

The conversation flowed. Janine told me about the shows that she'd appeared in and that she was contracted to the President Hotel until the end of the year and thought of going to LA after to find a decent agent. Maybe get into the film business, who knows?

We talked about New York, where she had learned to dance, act, and even sing, and how she grew up in San Diego.

"I'd love to return and visit my old home. Maybe on my next vacation, we could drive down there. It's a long time since I visited the Zoo and the Wild Animal Park."

I agreed, "Yeah, it's beautiful down there, the ideal climate, so let me know when you're in this neck of the woods again, and it's a date!"

Then Nat came over to where we were seated. The time had flown by. "It's one o'clock, and I'm up early tomorrow. You don't mind if we leave now, do you?" Nat asked me.

"Okay," I said.

And with that, Janine and I rose and said goodbye to the people there and to Beverley, Nat's girlfriend, thanking her for a wonderful evening.

"Well, I didn't see much of you two," she said, "but I guess you hit it off! Next time, Jeff, we'll have a chat."

We drove along the Pacific Coast Highway to Janine's hotel, where I said goodbye at the entrance, gave her my cell phone number, and asked her to call me when she knew she was coming to Laguna Beach next time.

We kissed, and as I got back to Nat's car, I called out, "Thanks for an amazing evening!"

****

My mind then turned to the present. I got out of my bed and made for the bathroom. I had a shower, made my bed, dressed, and made for the kitchen, where I found my mother and father on the terrace reading the Sunday papers.

"Hi, son, seems you had a good time last night. Don't you remember you said that we should come over at midday for lunch, and we rang your bell, but you didn't answer it? We thought you might be asleep, so we let ourselves in."

I must have been in the shower when they rang my doorbell, but quite honestly, I forgot they were coming over—*not that I minded.*

My mother said she was cooking something for us to eat, which would be ready in half an hour.

When she returned to the kitchen and with my father engrossed in the papers, I wandered over to the rail to glance at the ocean.

My mind drifted with thoughts of last night and, at the same time, of Italy and Maria.

This weekend, it was the first time in ages that I had thought of her as the job that I had kept me busy during the week, and my friends kept me busy during the weekends.

Life was now good to me. I was back to peak fitness, and even my sex life had improved. But how did Janine compare with Maria?

CHAPTER 6

The days turned to weeks, then months. Christmas came and went, and eventually, New Year's Eve arrived.

Out of the blue, my cell phone rang, and I was surprised but pleased that it was Janine on the line.

"Hi, Jeff, how are you doing?"

"Oh, this is a surprise."

"I thought I'd give you a call. My show has finished at last and next Sunday, I'm off to the U.K. I've been asked to audition for a show in London, so I'm very excited about it! I was wondering if I could come and visit you for four days and fly down to Orange Airport this afternoon if you like?"

"Great, I was going to a New Year's Eve party at Nat's new apartment, but I'm sure one extra person won't make any difference. Also, you can stay at my beach house, so you won't need to find a hotel. What time is your flight?"

"I can take one to arrive at Orange at 2 p.m."

"Great, I'll be there to pick you up. See you then."

Just after two, Janine walked through the arrival lounge with her two large suitcases. I hugged her, got hold of the trolley, put her cases on it, and made our way to where my car was parked.

A couple of hours later, we were in my house, sitting on the terrace, which led out to the beach, sipping two pina coladas. Janine looked amazing. I asked if her parents were still in San Diego.

"No, in fact, my father passed away when I was only nine. My mother remarried fifteen years ago and now lives in San Fransisco. You may be interested to know my mother is Jewish, as I can see you wear a Mogen Dovid on a chain around your neck."

"That makes you Jewish," I told her.

"Yes, I know, but I have only been to the Conservative Temple a few times, and with the life I lead, taking time off for the High Holy Days is always a problem. My mother tries to keep it, and whenever I visit her, you can guess I have a traditional Friday night feast, and by the time I have left, I am on a strict diet again!"

"I'm not that religious either, but every Friday evening, I attend my parents' home. It's nice, and I enjoy it. Sometimes, with my two brothers, their wives, my sister, and my nephews and nieces, it's quite a gathering! I'll have to get you invited!"

"I'd like that, but I'll make sure I'm wearing something more presentable," Janine joked, smiling, as she was sitting there with nothing on except a thong, which left nothing to the imagination.

We decided to go for a swim and made our way down the sand to the sea. A quick run and dive into the water, and we were both enjoying the California weather even more.

Janine was a great swimmer. She swam like a fish. One minute, she was floating on her back, and the next minute, diving into the waves and swimming under the water.

For a second, I lost her, and at the next moment, I felt a hand on my swim shorts from below the waves, and then they were being pulled down with a quick tug.

Her hands were now on my lower half—had the sea been crowded with bathers, nobody would have known what was going on!

It was an amazing experience what happened next.

I had now lost my swim shorts, and when it was time to come out of the sea, I said to her, "How am I going to get out of the water?"

"Well, since there are only one or two bathers around now, you'll have to make a dash for it. Or, you can stay here until the sun goes down!"

With the thought of being stung by a jellyfish on my private parts or one or two people seeing me naked for a minute, I decided on the former.

"Right, I'm coming out, I'll meet you on my terrace where I left my towel!"

I ran like a streaker in record time up the beach to my house with Janine laughing and chasing after me.

One minute later, I had reached the safety zone, my large white towel around my waist. Janine, still laughing, made her way toward me, reminding me of the scene where Ursula Andress came out of the sea in the movie 'Dr. No.'

She finally reached me, still in hysterics, and put her arms around me. Then we lay down on the large sun loungers facing the azure ocean, casually holding hands.

I felt good being with her, as she did things that not only were different but made me laugh! Then she let go of my hand, turned on her side, and opened the towel tucked into my waist.

I closed my eyes as I felt her hand on my leg and moving up in a northerly direction. It was not long before we were making love again. I thought I was fit, but where did Janine get the stamina from?

An hour later, we showered together, joking and still laughing at my 'streak' across the sand. We dried ourselves and got dressed. Although, at first, I could not see the necessity, but then there was a slight chance that my mother might suddenly pop in.

After relaxing with a cold beer, Janine laid out her clothes on our bed for the New Year's Eve party, then sat at the dressing table to blow dry her hair.

She picked out a gold lurex halter-necked top and matching pants.

I felt underdressed whatever I wore, but eventually settled on a white jacket, black voile shirt, and black pants and shoes.

When she finally was dressed, she looked like a goddess, the lurex top cut in a 'V' shape down to her navel, and her 'hipster' pants showing off her bare midriff.

We arrived at Nat's at nine to find some twenty people already there. Some we already knew from the party at Beverley's and a couple I knew from work.

Nat greeted us warmly, and I handed him a bottle of champagne I had brought with us. Soon, we were enjoying the food—which he decided to have catered— and the drinks and music.

It seemed that no one could take their eyes off Janine, and I felt good that she was with me. As it was Thursday, and three days later, on Sunday, she was flying off to London, I had to make the most of our time together.

The time seemed to speed by.

At 11.59 p.m., everybody was standing there with a glass of champagne in their hands, and at midnight, the radio chimed in the New Year.

We kissed passionately for a whole minute and, in turn, kissed our friends and wished them a 'Happy New Year.'

We then danced for some time, and then I said, "Let's go and finish off the celebrations at my place."

Not so long later, we were both under my shower, our clothes lying all over my bedroom carpet. The hot water rippled over our shoulders as we embraced, my hardness becoming apparent every second. Her hands were now sponging me down with soap as I stood facing her.

This was the best New Year's Eve that I could remember.

After we came out of the shower, we dried each other off, made wonderful love, and fell asleep in each other's arms.

I woke up at about nine-thirty and phoned my parents to wish them a happy new year, and at the same time, got an invite to come to dinner to celebrate the Sabbath since it was Friday.

Janine had got up while I had been on the phone, so we both had a shower, got dressed, and had something light to eat with some coffee.

"Come, I want to take you into the town as there's something I want to buy you."

"And what might that be?"

"You'll have to wait and see," I replied.

CHAPTER 7

When my mother invited me over for 'Shabbes' dinner, I told her about Janine.

"Well, ask her as well, 'hon.' There's only going to be us, as the rest of the family, as you know, are away. What's her name?"

"Janine," I answered, "and before you put your foot in it, she is Jewish on her mother's side."

"No problem, son, we'll see you at eight, and don't be late!"

Earlier that day, I had taken Janine to the shopping mall, and although it was New Year's Day, my friend, Bernie Martin, still had his jewellery store open.

It was only a twenty-minute walk to get there, and as usual, the sun was shining brightly, and the sea air was refreshing.

"Good morning, Bernie. A Happy New Year to you!"

"Oh, hi Jeff, how are you, and who's this gorgeous lady you're with?"

Bernie was a family man. In his late sixties, with hardly any hair on his head, he enjoyed his food, as his pants were never around his waist. He was wearing a white shirt, tie, and sports coat, and you could see he enjoyed his work as he always had a smile on his face.

He gave the personal touch, and his reputation was known for some distance along the Pacific Coast, from San Fransisco to San Diego.

He lived in Laguna Woods and had a beautiful two-bedroom condominium, which he shared with his wife, Linda. His two daughters, whom I went to high school with, now lived on the East Coast with their respective families and paid Bernie and Linda a visit at least twice a year.

"And what can I do for you this bright and new year morning?"

"You have in the window a small gold 'mezuzah." Can I have a look at it, please?"

Bernie stepped into his shop window and carefully took out a tray from the display. It held a thin piece of gold, about two inches long, attached to a gold chain.

I told Janine that a mezuzah is normally fixed to the front doorpost of a Jewish home, as well as on the doorposts of rooms inside the home. "It contains some prayers as well. This particular one is to wear round the neck. It will suit yours perfectly."

Stanley passed it to me.

"Put your head forward so I can fix it round your neck. There, that's it!"

Janine put her head back and looked in the mirror that Bernie was holding in front of her.

"It's lovely, but why? It's not my birthday."

"You've brought back the fun into my life again, and even if it's for a short time, while you're away in London, you will wear it when you can, and it will remind you of the time you spent with me, and moreover, that you are Jewish."

Janine hugged me.

"Leave it on," I said.

"I'll never take it off unless I have to!" Janine answered with tears in her eyes.

I then paid Bernie, and we both thanked him and said goodbye, walked out into the street, and began our journey to where my home was.

When we arrived back at my front door, I pointed out to Janine the mezuzah on the right side of the door post. "My parents have one on every door in their house, but for me, this one's good enough."

Then, I got the car out of the garage and drove fifteen minutes down the road to Dana Point, where there was a picturesque marina, fine boutiques, and a deli, which I hoped was open.

We parked the car, and as we walked around the marina, I could see the door open to 'Diane's Deli' and queues gathering. We found a spare table for two, and Janine stayed there while I went to order some food.

When it was my turn, it was Diane who served me.

"Hi, Di," I said, "a Happy New Year to you!"

Diane, an old friend, attractive and vivacious with short blonde hair, whom my family had known for years, greeted me with, "The same to you, and should I say hero as well?"

She took my order of two corned beef sandwiches on rye, a cucumber, and two lemon teas, and that would suffice until a visit to Mom's later on.

The food was delicious. We tucked into the sandwiches, which were hot, thick, and had hardly any fat on them, and then we washed them down with the tea.

Then we left, walked around the marina to our car, and made for home, where we sunbathed for the rest of the afternoon.

At ten to eight, we were ready for the visit to my parents.

Janine had put on a pair of pale blue jersey pants, with a white polo neck sweater covering her ample form. I was happy to just wear a pair of jeans with a blue striped shirt, and since my parents didn't stand on ceremonies, I knew that Janine would feel at home.

I picked up my 'yamulka' for my head, which I always wore at my parents for the Friday night service.

I found it in the kitchen drawer, then held Janine's hand, and we walked to my front door to leave.

Ten minutes later, we were outside the front door, where I rang the bell and waited patiently for it to open.

One minute later, it opened, and there stood my mother, still with her kitchen apron on to greet us.

"Welcome, come in, Janine, and make yourself at home!"

I kissed my mother on the cheek, and Janine did the same. Then we entered, wiped our shoes carefully on the mat, and followed my mother down the spiral staircase to the bottom level, where one of the lounges was near the kitchen.

My father rose from his chair. "Hi, son, and welcome, Janine, to the Gold family abode," he said, hugging us both before we sat down. "My, my! Jeff, you always have such good taste, but, Janine, you're exceptional!"

Janine, a little embarrassed, replied, "Well, thanks, Mr. Gold, you too look pretty good yourself!"

"Now, now, David, don't get any ideas," Mom said, chuckling to herself. "Now, can I offer you a drink, honey?"

"Nothing, thank you, Mrs. Gold, but I am looking forward to the meal, as I don't get a chance too often to celebrate the Sabbath 'cause I'm usually working."

"What exactly do you do?" my mother enquired.

"I'm in show business. I've been appearing in Las Vegas, and I'm off to London on Sunday afternoon. I've got an audition for a new musical there."

My father sat quietly, taking it all in, while my mother did the 'interrogating,' like Jewish mothers would!

"And what line of show business is that, my dear?"

"I studied drama and singing in New York, so I am after a major role in this new production."

"That sounds very interesting, and I wish you lots of luck with it!"

My mother, the typical Jewish mother, I thought. *Next thing, she'll want to know what her parents do!*

My father interrupted, thank goodness. "Sandy, isn't dinner ready yet? I'm sure Jeff and Janine are hungry?"

With that, my mother got up from where she was sitting and left for the kitchen.

"Sorry about that, Janine; she didn't mean any harm."

"Nothing taken, Mr. Gold."

"Call me David, please…"

A loud call came from the next room, "Dinner is served!"

We entered the large dining room. While we were still standing by our chairs, my mother lit the Sabbath candles in the usual custom and said a prayer.

My dad said a few more blessings, which included one for wine and one for the challah bread, and finally, we sat down.

Janine reminded me to cover my head just in time, and I took my yamulka out of my pocket and placed it on the back of my head.

Then my mother went into the kitchen and returned with a trolley containing some dishes of piping hot chicken soup. Then followed the roast chicken, roast potatoes, and greens, ending with fruit salad.

After the meal, we went out onto the terrace to relax. It was a lovely January evening, and the conversation was flowing. Soon, it was ten-thirty, and Janine whispered in my ear that we should go as she didn't want to outstay her welcome.

"Well, Mom and Dad, we're going to leave now as it's getting late," I said, and the four of us got up.

"It's been a lovely evening," Janine remarked.

"It's been a pleasure!" my father replied.

And my mother said, "You must come again the next time you're in California. We both wish you a safe trip to London and good luck with the audition!"

We made our way to the stairs and up to the front door; we embraced my parents and left for my beach house.

"You have great parents, Jeff. They made me so welcome. I felt like one of the family."

"I'm glad you got on with them so well. I don't take many ladies home to meet the parents!"

"Oh, I'm very flattered," she said and kissed me on the cheek.

Back at my house, we got undressed, washed, and then got into bed. We made love, fell asleep, and didn't wake up until nine-thirty the next morning.

Janine rose up before me. I sat up, rested on my right elbow, and watched Janine walk around the place, totally naked without a care in the world and totally oblivious to me, humming the music from the CD she had put on.

She then returned to the bedroom with toast and hot coffee for both of us, which she carefully took outside onto the terrace, just outside the patio doors she had opened earlier.

I got up, grabbed my shorts, skipped into the bathroom, and was back two minutes later to have breakfast.

We sat opposite each other without a care in the world, Janine's ample breasts resting on the table facing me.

"Are you trying to put me off my breakfast?"

"Of course not, Sugar," she replied, moving back from the table in her chair and letting her breasts disappear under the table.

"You're great fun, Janine. I haven't felt like this in ages! I don't know what I'll do when you leave tomorrow. It took me long enough to get over Maria, and now, I can hear the song on your CD called '*You Make Me Feel Brand New.*'"

"Oh, Sugar, you know I have my career to think of, and I'm not ready to settle down. If I get the part in London, it will be a minimum of a year's contract, so unless you come to visit me, I can't say what our future is."

Janine thought for a moment and continued, "I'm very fond of you, Jeff. You're fun to be with; you have a wonderful family and a nice, steady job. We could write to each other by email or telephone, but I don't really want a serious relationship at this time in my career. I'm sure you understand?"

CHAPTER 8

It was Monday, and I was at college and changing to take the seventeen-year-olds out for a jog around the soccer field.

While I was zipping my tracksuit, my thoughts went to Janine, who was now in London. I had taken her to Los Angeles Airport yesterday, and we had said our 'farewells.' She said she would contact me this evening, but being eight hours ahead of me in time, I didn't really expect it.

I had realized that she was right and had to put her career first. Who knows, she might make it to the top and have her name up in lights that would say, 'Janine Grey.' It was not likely to say 'Janine Gold.'

She did actually send me an email to say that she arrived safely and was shattered from a long flight and now jet lag.

The days, weeks, and months went by, and the phone calls, letters and emails, which were infrequent, became less and less. Janine was successful with her audition and now had a major part in a London musical.

Winter turned to spring, then summer, and then it was fall. I had a few dates here and there, but nothing to talk about. Janine became a thing of the past, just a happy memory.

Almost four years after I had returned from Italy, my father decided to retire from the business and put Gary in charge. Fortunately, he was able to continue his comfortable life due to good planning for his future, and his investments had been successful.

It was now September, and it was a Saturday morning, with the weather a little cooler for the time of year. I had driven up the coast to Newport Beach and had decided to visit Fashion Island in order to buy something for my mother's birthday next week. I parked my car in the car park and casually wandered towards the entrance of the shopping mall.

It was beginning to get crowded when, in the distance, I saw a young woman with dark hair pushing a child's buggy and entering a restaurant.

I could only see her from the side, but her face was distinctly familiar, and although she was walking to the other side of a large circular restaurant, something inside wanted me to take a closer look.

As I got nearer, I saw her get into a queue to buy some food at one of the many places that sold pasta. I noticed that the child must have been maybe three or four years old and had jet-black hair.

I was now some fifty feet away when she turned to go to find a vacant table with the food she had bought.

My heart suddenly started to beat quickly. This didn't seem possible, but I was pretty sure who she was.

I hid behind a vending machine, waiting for her to look up. My heart was at 'fast speed,' and I didn't know what to do?

And then she looked up. I was certain I was right. It was MARIA!

Then I remembered that she had told me she had some friends in California, but then I wondered whose child he was?

I just stood there. I had a frog in my throat, and it all came back to me.

It was some four years since I had said goodbye to her, but in a span of five minutes, that old feeling was returning. I put my sunglasses on, which were in my breast pocket, and wandered over to the kiosk where I bought a corned beef sandwich and a diet coke and turned to find a table.

Very fortunately, there was a table right next to hers, so I made my way to it and sat down, not looking up or in her direction to make it look like I was staring at her.

Then, out of the blue, she spoke.

"Excuse me, but do you have the correct time?"

"Just before one," I said, and by then, I couldn't stand it any longer and removed my sunglasses.

She looked as if she had seen a ghost!

"Maria, *come sta*?" I said quietly.

She nearly dropped her cup but somehow managed to put it down on the saucer.

"*Va bene, e lei?*" she replied hesitantly, now quite embarrassed.

"How are you, and how long have you been here?"

"Two weeks, but it was over between us, Jeff; we were from two different worlds."

I looked at the child sitting there in the buggy, smiling back at me, and I could see myself—he was just like me when I was a child!

"Maria, is this your child?"

"Yes, Jeff, this is Giovanni, and he is nearly four."

I was waiting for her to say who the father was, but she didn't volunteer the information.

"How is your mother and the rest of your family?"

"My mother passed away two years ago, but the rest of my family are well."

"Oh, I'm very sorry to hear about your mother."

Giovanni stretched his hand towards me as if he wanted me to take him, and Maria undid the straps and lifted him out, but at that moment, a man appeared and fondly kissed Maria and the child on their cheeks.

Maria asked him to sit down and said, "This is Neil; Neil, this is Jeff."

He shook my hand. "Pleased to meet you," he said. "Are you two old friends?"

Maria butted in before I could answer. "This is the man I told you whom I looked after in a hospital in Milano."

"Oh yes, the war hero!" Neil said rather sarcastically.

"How long have you known each other?" I asked.

"Just over a year. We met in San Francisco at a friend's party, and we've been together ever since."

For some reason, I took a dislike to Neil, and I could see that Maria felt very awkward.

"How long are you in California for, Maria? Maybe we could meet up someplace as I've got to go now," I said as I looked at my watch.

"I'll give you a ring, Jeff. Let me have your cell phone number."

I got out a pen I luckily had in my jacket and wrote down the number on a serviette for her, and as she bent down to put the number away, I noticed she was still wearing the Mogen Dovid I bought her.

I got up, kissed Maria on the cheek, shook Neil's hand, and called out to Giovanni, "Ciao, Giovanni." I said goodbye and left.

As I walked toward the exit, I kept on looking back, and I could see what looked like an argument taking place between Neil and Maria. Then I saw Neil get up and walk off, and he seemed in a temper.

I made for the bookstore and bought myself a new soccer magazine that I liked to read, then made my way to Carole's Fashion Boutique outside to see what I could buy for my mother.

I settled for a beautiful silk scarf in a multitude of colors that I knew my mother would like. Then I walked back to my car, and as I got to the parking lot, I saw Maria again. She was alone with Giovanni, and I wondered where Neil had gone to.

I drove south on the highway but could not take my mind off Maria and her boy.

When I arrived home, I changed into my shorts, picked up my towel, suntan lotion, and the magazine I had bought and walked out of the patio doors, where I sat on my lounger and started to read.

The trouble was, I couldn't read a line without thinking of Maria and the past, reliving every wonderful memory. I realized that I still loved her.

I thought of the last time we made love. *Did she get pregnant?*

Was Giovanni Italian for Jeff?

He is definitely my son!

CHAPTER 9

Maria had rented a two-bedroom apartment in Venice Beach. It wasn't big, but it was comfortable and was near the seafront.

She shared it with Neil, her son, and her nanny, and although Neil knew that Giovanni wasn't his, he loved the boy like he was his.

Maria and Neil had first met at Neil's friend's party just over a year ago. Neil had literally bumped into Maria in a crowded room, and then and there, they started talking.

They found two vacant seats and commenced a long conversation, which included that Maria had a two-and-a-half-year-old son.

Neil expected the father to come up to him and demand what Neil was doing talking to his 'partner,' but no one came, and after they had introduced themselves to each other, Maria said, "I am a single mother."

Nothing more was said about it. It was not Neil's business to ask, and he was entranced by her good looks. Neil managed a sports shop along the beachfront, and it was always packed with surfers buying the latest surfboards and equipment. He had the choice of many young 'beach babes' and had dated quite a few, but none of them meant much to him.

Maria was different. She had an innocence about her, yet there was a certain mystery that attracted him to her.

Maria had acquired a position at the Los Angeles General Hospital two months after her mother had passed on. It was sad, and it took time to sort everything out. With the help of her brothers and close friends, the funeral took place in the local church in Stresa, and it was her old friend, Father Giancarlo, who officiated.

There were many people there to pay their respects to the wonderful lady, and when it was over, Maria's brothers took care of all the family affairs. The wine business was still flourishing nicely, and soon, everything was back to normal.

In Signora Carlotti's Will, though, she had left a large sum of money to Maria as well as her sons, which Maria was very grateful for.

One morning, a short while before she went to America, she found herself feeling sick and late for her period, and she guessed that she might be pregnant.

A hospital test proved that she was correct and she found it difficult to keep it to herself. As much as she was liked, a baby out of wedlock was frowned upon, and Maria thought it was best to move away.

Just by chance, she saw an advert in the Milan Medical Journal that a head of development was wanted in Los Angeles, U.S.A., and with all the qualifications that were asked for, Maria fitted the bill perfectly.

She went to see Doctor Rossi and told him that she was going to apply for the job, which came with an amazing salary, and asked if he would help her.

"*Certo, Mia Cara*, of course, my dear, if you wish to use my computer, let me know."

Maria had confided in Doctor Rossi about her pregnancy, and he was shocked. He loved Maria like his own daughter and had helped to bring her into the world. He did say, though, that she should tell her family and that they would accept the situation even though they wouldn't be too happy.

Of course, Father Giancarlo had to be told when Maria went to confession, but once again, although he knew it was a sin to do what she did, he said he would bless the child when he saw it.

Six months later, Maria gave birth to a son, and called it Giovanni, and he looked just like his father.

So it came to pass that Maria was given the job in America. The interviews took place via the Internet, and the panel that interviewed her were extremely impressed with her and her references. Maria said goodbye to her colleagues at the hospital, her family, and her friends. It was a tearful occasion.

Los Angeles was over six thousand miles away, but with the telephone and now the Internet, it took seconds to contact whoever she wanted to. She just had to remember the nine-hour time difference.

CHAPTER 10

She settled down in the Los Angeles General Hospital, and was put in charge of a whole floor, made up of four wards, with mainly private rooms.

Her boss was a Doctor Stanley, a senior consultant who was the chief administrator in the hospital.

The hours were fairly good to her. Eight until four, six days a week, and every other weekend off. There were staff to cover her absence, and from the beginning, she was liked by everyone, including the patients.

When she told Doctor Stanley and the rest of the team that interviewed her that she had a child and that she was a single mother, they weren't too pleased. But she told them that she had a full-time nanny who was like one of her family, so the child wouldn't interfere with her job. The doctors were so impressed with her CV, as, in fact, they had never seen such good references from the Milan hospital, and they would have been fools to turn her down!

There had been many who were qualified for the job, but Maria had the 'X' factor, and Doctor Stanley knew that Maria was the right choice.

Even with a baby, she was always punctual, and with help from Neil and her nanny, she was so happy with life, and everything seemed perfect.

Then things started to go wrong as Neil said that he was always very busy at the sports shop and wasn't arriving home until much later than usual. He claimed that it was because the shop was staying open for extra hours during the summer season. He was selling all the latest surfboards like hot cakes and, therefore, kept the place open longer.

He seemed to spend less time looking after Giovanni, and one evening, Maria overheard a telephone conversation that sounded as if he was speaking to a woman.

Maria decided to say nothing. It could be business, but when they went to bed, she knew something was up, as sex was going from every night to just once a week. The usual excuses, but they didn't work with Maria, and she decided to do something about it.

CHAPTER 11

On the day that Neil was working late to do what he claimed was stock-taking—and on this particular day, he always came home late—Maria, who knew she had a spare set of keys to his shop hanging in her apartment hallway, decided to pay him an unexpected visit.

She told her nanny that she was going out for a few hours, and when it was getting dusk, she called for her close friend, Lucy, whom she had confided in, and they drove to Neil's shop and parked the car.

Although the front of the shop was dark, there was a side entrance to the back, which was fortunately open, and they carefully walked around to where there was a small window.

There was a small light on, and very slowly, they peered through the window and there on a mattress were two naked bodies. A young blonde girl was on top, and Neil was underneath, facing her.

Maria was not shocked, as she expected something like this, so they returned to the front of the shop, where they decided what to do next. Maria took out from her pocket the spare key and very quietly opened the door.

The two of them walked towards the door at the back. When they got there, they quickly pushed it open and walked into the room. Both Neil and the girl had the shock of their lives. The girl screamed and grabbed the nearest item to cover herself up while Neil sat up and looked as if he had seen a ghost.

He gasped, looked at Maria in shock, and said, "I can explain!" Which, of course, he couldn't!

Maria, in a calm manner, said, "You have twenty-four hours to take all your belongings and get out! I want your door key now, and tomorrow, which is Saturday, you can come and collect everything!"

"But I need more time to find somewhere to stay?"

"I'm sure one of your many beach babes will be too happy for you to stay there! I'm not working tomorrow, so I will be there when you come. Giovanni will be out for the day, so it will be just me there. I have already spoken to my lawyer, who said you are not entitled to anything. You have no excuses, and all the flowers you might bring with you for me, in order to make up, will go in the trash can!"

Neil got up, grabbed a towel to cover himself, and found the apartment keys, handing them to Maria, who then turned with Lucy and walked out of the door to the front entrance and then to the road where her car was parked.

"Thank goodness that's all over, and thank you, Lucy, for coming with me. I don't think I could have done it on my own!"

Maria drove Lucy home and then returned to her apartment. Revenge had been sweet!

CHAPTER 12

The following morning, Neil had arranged for a friend to work in the shop for a few hours until he returned and then hired a van and drove it to Maria's.

She opened the door to him, and he found that she had already put his clothes from his closet on the sofa and armchairs for him to remove. It was fortunate that Maria's apartment was on the ground floor, as it made it easier for Neil to take everything out. After they were put in the van, he collected his hi-fi equipment and all other electrical goods that were his, then his stuff from the bathroom, and he was ready to leave.

Maria told him that if anything else turned up, she would let him know. Also, there was a court order that stated that he wasn't allowed to see Giovanni for any reason.

Neil filled up the van and returned for the last time to the apartment to say goodbye, but Maria stepped back when he tried to kiss her and just said, "Leave!"

There was nothing more to say, but when she closed the door, she sat down on the sofa and cried. They had been so happy. She knew how much Giovanni liked him, and now this!

She thought for a moment about Jeff. She had his cellphone number, but no, she didn't need anyone in her life at that moment!

How was she going to explain this to Carmen, her nanny, and Giovanni?

But then, as one door closes, another opens...

CHAPTER 13

One morning, who should have walked into Maria's office at the hospital,` but Gerry Davis, who was the chief fundraiser for the California Heart Foundation and was organizing the annual gala fundraiser taking place later that month at the New Kings Hotel in Newport Beach.

The hospital board of management had two tables, and even though the tickets were $200 each, Gerry had generously bought Maria a ticket to sit at his table.

He said that not only was she well-liked at the hospital, but her good work for the foundation was being recognized by many prominent people in high places throughout the State of California.

"Hi, Maria, how are ya doin?

"Come sta? Va bene, Gerry, e lei?"

Gerry, who only knew a few words in Italian, thought it wiser to continue the conversation in English.

"I feel just great, especially after seeing a beautiful gal like you first thing in the morning and telling you that we've sold four hundred tickets!"

"Wonderful, Gerry, that's $80,000! If you see someone in the finance department on the top floor, they'll give you a cheque for the two hospital tables!"

"It should be better than ever this year, and the new ballroom looks out onto the Pacific with the most amazing floodlit terrace. We have three bands, one of which is Latin American and a well-known American Italian singer who has just completed a stint at Carnegie Hall. He is giving his services for free. I won't say who it is, as it will be a surprise to everyone there, but I'm quite sure we should reach our million-dollar target hopefully by the end of the evening, and possibly much more!"

Maria was also looking forward to it and had decided on her next day off to go up to Fashion Island in Newport Beach to look for a suitable evening dress.

Just then, the phone went, and it was a doctor in one of her wards, asking if she could pay him a visit.

"Sorry, Gerry, I have to go and see someone now."

Gerry rose from his seat, held out his hand to Maria, and as she bent forward, he kissed her on the cheek.

Maria knew Gerry had a soft spot for her, although he was in his fifties and a widower.

He had made his money in oil when, as a young man, he and his late father lived in Houston and ran one of the biggest oil refineries in Texas.

Now retired, he had a home in Beverly Hills and owned a couple of hotels, the main one being the Clarence Beach Hotel in Miami.

His mother had died when he was just fourteen, and his wife had died some twelve years ago with heart problems.

He had to bring up a son and a daughter when they were quite young, not entirely on his own, as there were many friends and staff caring for his two teenagers. In those days, he was working sixteen hours a day, and the kids, Jonathan and Jessica, got used to it.

But now, he took it easy. He sold the refinery and invested his money in real estate, and both his children were executives in the business, which included the two hotels.

"Hope to see you soon," he said as he left the room.

On Maria's next day off, she drove to Newport Beach in order to purchase a suitable gown for the big event.

CHAPTER 14

David and Sandy Gold were sitting around their dining room table on the eve of the biggest charity function of the year. The Heart Foundation Charity, they always attended, and this one in California had to be the best.

They had sold tickets for five tables themselves. Close friends and business associates had all come forward to join them, and Gerry Davis had been David's client and close friend for over forty years. They had spoken regularly about the functions and were looking forward to seeing each other there.

There was a table for David's sons, Gary, Michael, and Jeff, and their wives and friends. Jeff, of course, was on his own, as there was no lady in his life at that moment, and since he had seen Maria the last time, he found it difficult to think of any other women.

The evening would begin with a champagne reception at 4.30 pm, which would be followed by a four-course meal an hour later. There would be a welcoming speech by the president of the California Heart Foundation, Dexter Miller, with others to follow later, when Dexter would introduce Gerry, who would make the appeal.

The dancing would commence after and continue until ten, when coffee and pastries would be served. Then there would be the cabaret and a surprise guest.

Then after that, more dancing until 2 a.m., and then, it would end with the 'last waltz.'

"Have you decided what you're going to wear, hon?" David said with a grin.

Sandy looked at him and replied, "What are you talking about? I'm wearing the emerald green gown with the necklace to go with it!"

"Well, you've been trying on dresses for the past month, and I'm sure your dress designer must be tired of coming backward and forward waiting for you to make up your mind if any alterations are required."

"I'm glad, David, you don't have all that trouble. Tell me, how many tuxedos did you try on?"

"How many do you think I have?"

The friendly banter went on for some time. They knew there were no bad feelings; it was just a bit of fun, which sometimes even led to their bedroom.

"I shall wear the black double-breasted, with the red bow that I can tie myself, and it will match your red lips, so come here and let me get a closer look."

"Sorry, hon, got to check my shoes and stockings!" And with that, Sandy got up and went out of the room.

David sat there for a while, staring through the large window at the Pacific Ocean, the moon casting a white path over the water.

Life has been good, he thought. Four wonderful children who had given Sandy and him such joy, and an angel for a wife, who was totally devoted to him.

With such stories he had heard about broken marriages, he was glad that he and Sandy were not part of the Orange County 'Jet Set.' Their marriage was made in heaven. They had been sweethearts from the first day they set eyes on each other in High School, and there had never been anyone else.

David eventually rose from his comfortable seat, switched off the lights, locked the doors, and went upstairs, where he was sure Sandy would be.

As he walked into the bedroom through the double doors, he noticed the emerald dress hanging up over the closet under a plastic cover, and neatly standing underneath were emerald green shoes to match.

David walked straight through to their ensuite bathroom, showered, and returned to the bedroom.

He turned back the bedspread and got into bed beside his beloved Sandy, now with no make-up on, but in his eyes, still beautiful.

He bent forward to kiss her on the cheek. "I love you, Sandy," he said.

"I love you, too, David," Sandy lovingly replied.

David switched off the lamp, lay down, and eventually went off to sleep.

CHAPTER 15

I returned from the beach after a restful afternoon swimming, sunbathing, and reading the latest Henry Tudor novel that had just come out.

Henry was a prolific writer. His last three books were not only best sellers, but were made into movies. They were thrillers with a touch of romance, and his latest, '*The Double Deal*,' was no exception.

I gathered my beach towel and bag containing the sun cream and book and walked back to my beach house door. I opened it with the code number and took my 'flip flops' off as I walked in.

I checked for messages on the phone, which were none, so I went to the bathroom and had a shower.

My life now was tied up with the new soccer team I had produced at college. Known as 'Laguna Lions,' they headed the league table of ten teams, which were all from colleges in California. The ages were from eighteen to twenty, and as professional soccer was becoming more popular now, scouts from top professional clubs came to watch our matches.

I came out of a cool shower, dried myself, put on a pair of shorts, and then sat down to watch the news on the television. Normally. I would go to my parents on a Friday night, but tonight I decided to give it a miss. It was 'pasta night' for a change, and I wanted to relax in my own company, as tomorrow was the main night of the year.

I put on the spaghetti, then cooked the meatballs my mother had made for me, and when it was ready, laid the table for one, then opened a bottle of California red wine. There were times when I preferred my own company, and tonight was definitely one of them.

When my meal was over, I put everything in the dishwasher, picked up my book, and went out onto the floodlit terrace where I sat down and made myself comfortable.

I was pretty happy with life now, but deep down would have liked to be able to share it with my own family. That made me think of my time in Milan and how I fell in love with Maria, and I wondered if she was still in California or if she had returned to Italy.

If only? I thought.

The following day, I just relaxed after doing a bit of housework, and then at three, I took a shower and got dressed for the big event later on.

At four o'clock, I locked my front door, got into my Mercedes Coupe parked in the drive, and drove to my parents' whom I was following to the 'do.'

"Hi, hon," my mother said as she opened the door for me.

I gave her a hug and told her how lovely she looked.

"You don't look too bad yourself, Jeff. Why you haven't been snapped up long ago beats me!"

I sat down in the living room and waited for my father to make his appearance.

"Hi, son, how ya doin?" he said as he walked into the room.

I got up, and he hugged me around the neck.

"Let's go, everyone!" he said.

My father got the Jag out of the garage. I opened the door for my mother to get in, then got into my own car to follow them.

The journey was a twenty-minute trip up the Pacific Highway coast road. As we got near the New Kings Hotel, there was a multitude of flags waving in the breeze, the cars queuing up, and the guests being helped out of their limos by doormen wearing long red tail coats and top hats. Then, other staff took their cars and parked them.

My mother, father, and I walked up the stone steps, passed the hotel reception, and followed the sign to the Royal Suite where the function was taking place. We showed our invitations to the security guy and entered a large banqueting suite lit up with magnificent chandeliers, with decorated tables at the far end of the room in front of a stage.

The champagne was flowing, and waiters in short red jackets were walking around, handing out drinks and canapes. My parents didn't eat those as they weren't 'kosher,' and, like many other guests, a vegetarian menu was provided for them.

After an hour of mingling with friends, dinner was announced. After I had checked the table plan, which was on an easel near the entrance to the room, I made it to where I was sitting.

I arrived at my table, where I joined Gary, Michael, and their beautiful wives and friends.

Eventually, when everyone was seated, the orchestra started playing, and the waiters and waitresses began to serve the first course of smoked salmon. This was followed by asparagus soup with croutons, and the main course was a choice of roast chicken, steak or fish, with assorted vegetables. The religious Jews were given baked halibut with lemon sauce, with creamed potatoes, peas, carrots, and it was all washed down with some Chablis.

After this, we were glad for a break, and after a welcoming speech by the president, he then introduced Gerry Davis, who came to the microphone, and made his appeal.

"My dear friends and patrons, it is my pleasure, as usual, to tell you all how pleased I am to welcome you to the main event of the year and say how wonderful it is to say hello to the most generous people in California."

After speaking for some twenty minutes about what the charity needed for funding for this year, and where the money would go, he eventually closed his speech to thunderous applause.

After the main course and dessert, it was almost time for the president to open the ball with his wife, so I excused myself from the table and got up and made my way to the exit to go to the washroom.

It was after I returned that I saw her.

Walking down the stairs toward her table in a white sequinned ball gown that shimmered in the light was Maria!

The dress was so elegant and cut in a 'V' shape at the front, barely covering her breasts. It fitted like a glove, and around her neck, she wore the Star of David that I had bought her when I had said goodbye in Milan.

Her hair was done up high and behind in curls, with a white ribbon and clasp holding it together. She could have been a princess, and I stood there transfixed, hypnotized—call it what you like.

She was the most beautiful creature I had ever seen! I watched her make her way back to her seat, to the far side of the banqueting hall, and that was probably why I hadn't seen her at the reception, though I imagined that she must have been surrounded by many gentlemen.

I got to my seat. My heart was pounding again, and I was dying to see who she was seated next to.

Then, the master of ceremonies announced that the president and his wife would now open the ball, and everybody applauded, as Ray Archer and his orchestra started playing the opening number.

CHAPTER 16

Soon, the dance floor was crowded, and the only person not dancing from my table was me!

I got up and looked to my left, and after scanning the room, I saw her! And she, too, was the only one at her table not dancing.

What do I have to lose? *I thought.* So, I then got up and made my way to her table. I came up to her from behind her so that she couldn't see me, then bent down to her ear, and whispered in Italian, *"Vuole ballare?"*— *Would you like to dance?*

Maria turned, and our eyes met. "Oh, my God! Jeff, what a lovely surprise! How come you're here?"

"If you dance with me, I will tell you," I told her, and then I offered my hand.

She stood up, smiled at me, and we made our way to the dance floor. Everyone seemed to turn to look at us, or perhaps it was her. All I know was that I felt like I was on 'cloud nine' just being in her presence. We danced to the slow 'fox trot,' which was called *'It had to be you*,' and I was holding Maria for the first time since that fateful day in Stresa.

I told her that my parents were on the committee and that I had come with them. She then told me how she had come to be there, and despite the music, we didn't stop talking.

The music changed to a more romantic number. It was an old Italian tune, and very well known, which my parents were fond of.

"Non dimenticar, means don't forget you are, my darling. Don't forget to be, all you mean to me..." the words went.

I put my arms around Maria, moving a little closer and then rested my head on her right cheek. Thank God she didn't pull away, and I was feeling so pleased that I had come tonight on my own!

"Where's Neil?" I asked.

"I'm no longer with Neil. I'm on my own, but tonight, my nanny is looking after Giovanni."

I didn't want to ask any more questions, but I was elated, on 'cloud nine,' and was wondering if this was fate? We were near the terrace, and since the door leading to it was open, I guided Maria outside.

We were the only ones there, and as we looked in front of us, we saw the beautiful floodlit gardens, and on the horizon, we could see the Pacific Ocean. We stood there in silence for a moment or two, then I turned Maria towards me, lifted her chin upwards, and said, "*Tu sei molto bella!*"

I then bent my head forward and kissed her slowly on the lips, not knowing how she would react. The slow kiss developed into a passionate embrace, and my emotions got the better of me.

"*Ti amo*, Maria; nothing has changed. This must be fate because you are living here and on your own now, and we met here tonight. This must be a sign that we were meant to be together. There must be a way for us to be together. Move in with me—I have enough room for you and Giovanni. I could even turn my study into a bedroom for him."

"*Non lo so*"—I don't know—"Jeff, I have always loved you. But I would have to think about it."

At that moment, who should come onto the terrace but Gerry Davis, who had to have a cigarette?

"Maria, and oh, Jeff," he said in surprise. "I didn't know that you knew each other?"

"Gerry, isn't it a small world? I was the nurse who looked after Jeff when he was in hospital in Milan, and this is the first time that I have seen him since I came to live in California!"

Maria thought it best not to mention that meeting at Fashion Island.

"Well, I have known Jeff since he was born, as his family and I are close friends. How extraordinary. Have you met Jeff's parents?"

"No, Gerry."

"Then now's the time to meet them! Come with me, both of you."

I don't think Maria and I wanted this to happen, but Gerry grabbed Maria's arm and led her, followed by me, back into the ballroom toward the table where my parents were seated.

"David and Sandy, look and see who I have found on the terrace!"

My mother and father looked up and saw a rather nervous young woman standing there with Gerry by her side and me just behind her.

"David, Sandy, I want to introduce you to the most beautiful young lady in Southern California!"

"I think we've met before?" my mother said.

"Well, actually, Mrs. Gold, I think I met you just once in Milan, when your son was in the hospital there. I was in Doctor Rossi's room at the time."

"Oh, yes, how could I forget such a beautiful face?"

My father interrupted, "What a gorgeous creature!"

Maria was now embarrassed, and I quickly stepped in to save her awkwardness.

"Mom and Dad, Maria looked after me during my stay in Milan. She was wonderful, and we became good friends. She even took me to visit her family in Stresa, whom I also became fond of, and then, when I left Milan and returned to California, I never thought I'd ever see her again. It's just by chance that she came to live in

California and went to work at the LA General Hospital."

"Well, Maria," my father said, "it's a pleasure meeting you. You've done a fantastic job on Jeff. How could we possibly repay you, without inviting you to our home?"

"You must come," my mother butted in, "and, of course, Jeff will bring you!"

Then it suddenly dawned on her who Maria was.

Gerry was now standing back while this exciting conversion took place, while Maria was really lost for words in English as well as Italian, and moreover, so was I. Was this really happening?

"Oh, thank you," Maria replied. "I will look forward to seeing you again, but now, please excuse me, as I have to return to my table"

My mother and father rose and kissed Maria goodbye on the cheek as if they were old friends, then I escorted Maria back to her table, while Gerry stayed with my parents.

As soon as Maria got there, she sat down, and I took hold of her hands.

"Meet me soon! When are you free? Please don't let this chance meeting end here, Maria. This was fate, and we were meant to meet again and be together!"

"I am free on Tuesday evening. I usually meet my friend, Lucy, for a meal, but I'm sure she will understand when I tell her about tonight, and we can postpone our date for another evening. I'll meet you at the Laguna Inn, Jeff, at eight o'clock. If I have any problems, I will phone you as soon as I have your cell phone number."

CHAPTER 17

It was now 3 a.m. David and Sandy were on their way home after a fabulous evening, but they couldn't get out of their minds the beautiful creature who came over to their table with Jeff and Gerry.

"How come, Sandy, Jeff never mentioned her before? It seems strange. Did you notice what she was wearing round her neck?"

"Yes. a Mogen Dovid, David,"

And David replied," A nice Jewish Italian girl from Milan! Just right for Jeff—it's about time he settled down!"

It suddenly dawned on Sandy that this might be the girl Jeff had poured out his heart about to her. *Oh Lord!* she thought silently. *What is he going to do?*

They eventually got into bed just before 4 a.m.

At Jeff's home, he also got into bed at the same time. But he just lay there, as he knew that he wouldn't sleep.

He closed his eyes and said, "*Shema Yisroel..*"—the Hebrew prayer he had said often during his childhood. "Hear, oh Israel, the Lord our God, the Lord is one!"

He then prayed in English. "Dear Lord, I pray that you have brought Maria and me together again for a purpose. To be with each other for good. I pray that my family will love her as much as I do, and that our religions will not stop us from being together. We both worship you in our own ways, and I will try to be a better Jew if you grant my wishes. I believe in fate, and I am sure this was meant to be. Amen."

Soon, the dawn broke, the sun rose in the sky, and a new day began. Jeff eventually fell asleep, but when he awoke, it was midday. He got up, showered, and made a cup of coffee for himself. He wasn't hungry and could only think of one thing.

Just after one o'clock, his phone rang, and he went over to where it was and picked up the receiver on the fourth ring.

"Hi, hon, are you okay? Dad and I have missed breakfast, probably like you, and I've got some fresh bagels; what do you say?"

"Thanks, Mom, that sounds nice, but I have a lot of tidying up to do. Maybe I'll call in later."

"Okay, son, speak to you soon."

The phone went 'click,' and Jeff replaced it on the receiver.

He didn't want to go to his parents as much as he liked fresh bagels, as he knew they'd start asking questions, which, at the moment, he didn't want to answer.

"He's not coming, David," Sandy called out to her husband. "He said he might call round later."

"Shame, I was going to ask him about Maria, this beauty that he never mentioned to us before. We'll have to ask them over on a Friday night."

When Maria arrived home, she crept into Giovanni's room to find him sound asleep. She then went to the bathroom and got ready for bed, but like Jeff, she, too, found it hard to sleep and wondered if it was fate that brought Jeff back into her life.

She eventually drifted into a deep sleep and woke up at nine-thirty, then put her dressing gown on and went to the kitchen to find Carmen, her Mexican nanny, having breakfast with Giovanni.

Carmen had been with Maria since Giovanni was born. She originally came from Mexico City, but was brought up most of her life in San Diego Old Town, where there was still a large Mexican community.

She had always wanted to look after children. After working in a nursery for five years, and having also learnt English at school, she applied to Maria's advert in the local nursing magazine when Giovanni was born.

She applied for the post, was interviewed, and with excellent references, was hired by Maria. She was wonderful with the baby and did her duties perfectly, not interfering with Maria's social life, and was always there when Maria had to work extra hours. Because of this, Maria paid her well and gave her time off whenever she needed it. Furthermore, Maria thought that when Giovanni was older, he would be able to speak Italian, English, and even Spanish! Some feat for a young child!

"Good morning—*buon giorno/buenos dias!*" Maria said in three languages. She said it as if she had won the American lottery.

"What a beautiful morning! What shall we do today?"

CHAPTER 18

It was Tuesday evening. I had recovered from the event on Saturday and returned to work yesterday—if that's what you call it, coaching a wonderful bunch of kids into the skills of 'soccer.'

I had arrived home just after six, which gave me time to have a shower and change for my date.

I had told my parents that I was meeting Maria, and they wished me a great evening, and at the same time, suggested that I ask Maria over one Friday night. This, I intended to discuss later, but I would just see how the evening went, as I didn't want to take anything for granted. For I knew, it might be an anti-climax, with nothing coming of it.

I left at seven thirty for the Laguna Inn, which was ten minutes up the coast.

I had put on a new pair of jeans I had recently bought, with a white shirt and a gray sports coat. The weather was still quite mild, so I kept the car roof down, drove up to the end of the road, and turned left onto the coastal highway. Then up the hill to where the shops were, I continued toward Newport Beach. I then turned right at the next set of lights and soon saw the yellow neon sign saying 'Laguna Inn.'

I had phoned in advance and had reserved a table for two. The 'Maitre D' knew me quite well, and I know he would find me a nice table in a secluded part of the restaurant.

I parked my car and walked through the entrance.

Jacques, who was French, saw me and greeted me, "Good evening, Monsieur Gold, nice to see you again. Follow me; your lady is waiting for you!"

I followed Jacques past the tables with their tartan linen tablecloths. The waiters, who were hurrying by serving other diners, were also wearing matching tartan waistcoats, and the place was lit with candles around the room.

Finally, I reached the table, which was at the end of three alcoves, and in the background, I could hear soft music, which had a continental flavour to it.

Maria, who was sitting there, rose and greeted me with a loving peck on the cheek. "*Ciao*, Jeff, *come va?*"

"*Va bene, e lei?*" I answered.

I sat down, and Jacques placed two menus in front of us, which included the wine list. "I'll be back shortly," he said and walked away, leaving us alone.

Maria was wearing a black sequinned top with black pants. Her hair was brushed over to the side in a casual look, and it was difficult not to take my eyes off her.

"How have you been, Maria? I'm pleased you could make it."

"I'm fine, thank you, Jeff."

"You look lovely, Maria, but then, it doesn't matter what you wear—you will always look good to me! How is Giovanni?"

"Oh, he's growing up fast and looks more like his father every day."

I knew in my mind what she would say next, and I wanted to mention it at some point in the evening.

Maria then moved closer to me and reached for my hands, and I could see a small tear appear in her eyes and fall down her beautiful face. She seemed troubled.

Maria looked searchingly into my eyes. Then, she said, "Giovanni is your son!"

I let go of her hands and put my arms around her. Then she broke away, and I could see that she was crying.

"I knew the first time I saw him, Maria, when I met you in Fashion Island. Giovanni was just like a picture that my parents had of me in their living room. I'm so glad you have told me, as I didn't want to ask you."

"Well, Jeff, you must understand it has been difficult. He was born in Milan, and I couldn't keep my pregnancy a secret. My family, of course, were not happy, as they are religious Catholics, but realized that it was something that they would have to accept, and so, they supported me as much as they could.

"After Giovanni was born, I stayed in Stresa with my family, and I thank God that my mother saw him before she passed away; she guessed that you were the father. I remember she said, '*Che sara, sara!*'—What will be, will be!'

"But it was one reason why I had to get away, and when the opportunity arose, I took it. It was time to start a new life. I could have contacted your family, but it would not have been fair. So, I hope that you will understand in time, and now you know. We will have to think about what we should do…"

I held Maria tight and said, "Don't worry, I feel thrilled and excited. Wait until my parents hear the news!"

"Oh, Jeff, it's not going to be that easy…"

At that moment, Jacques returned to take our orders. We had forgotten about the food, so I quickly opened up the menu. "What would you like, Maria?"

"I'll have the minestrone, followed by the sole meuniere with sauté potatoes and an assortment of vegetables."

"That sounds good, I'll have the same," I said.

Jacques wrote it down and asked if we would like anything to drink, and I said that a small bottle of

Californian white wine would be fine. When Jacques left, we continued with our conversation about our son.

"Maria, I want to give you some money for Giovanni on a regular basis. You must give me your bank details. Also, when can I see him? In the last ten minutes, I feel quite different!"

"Next Saturday, I'm taking him to the beach just across the road from where I live. How about you meet me there at two?

"Okay, that'll be great. I'll look forward to it."

Soon, our meal arrived. We were both hungry, and the food was devoured with haste and washed down with some wine.

We didn't stop talking. I wanted to know everything Maria had done since our parting in Italy.

The evening went too quickly. Soon it was eleven o'clock, and it was time to leave.

I paid the cheque, and we made our way to Maria's car when she opened the door, and turned to me.

"Thank you for a lovely evening. I will look forward to Saturday." I put my arms around her. "*Ti amo*," I said and kissed her on her lips.

She responded and replied, "*Ti amo*, Jeff, I suppose I always have. *Ci vediamo sabato*"—*see you on Saturday.*

She got into the car. I closed the door for her, and she drove away.

CHAPTER 19

I realized when I arrived home that I had not mentioned Friday night, but I decided that it should happen another time and not the coming Friday.

I slept well and couldn't wait for Saturday to come. The rest of the week seemed to get better and better. I sent a message to my parents that Maria wouldn't be coming.

Soon, Friday afternoon came, and I popped by my parents' on the way home from work.

I pressed the front doorbell, then the code, and the door opened.

"Hi, Mom," I called and made my way down the spiral stairs to the ground floor where I knew my mother would be.

"Hello, son," she said as she walked out of the kitchen and then greeted me with a loving peck on my cheek. "How's your week been and how did you get on Tuesday night?"

"It was really nice actually, but about tonight, Maria is working, as she has tomorrow off, and myself—I have to catch up on some paperwork, so unfortunately, I'm sorry but I won't be coming either. Training soccer players all week doesn't mean I don't have to read books or write papers.

"I'm seeing Maria and her little son, Giovanni, tomorrow, and we'll be going to the beach, so I'll ask her then if she's free to come one Friday night. How's Dad?"

"He's fine. He went over to Gary's to see the grandchildren, but he'll be home soon."

I wondered if my mother said that for a reason, like she would hope to have grandchildren by me? It was ironic as she DID and didn't know it!

"I've got an idea, Jeff. Why don't you all come to tea about four-thirty tomorrow, when you come off the beach?"

"Well, I don't know what Maria's plans are afterwards. I'll phone her later and ask her, and I'll pop by tomorrow after you've returned from the temple and let you know."

With that, I kissed my mother goodbye and made my way up the stairs to the front door. I turned the knob and walked over to my car, and ten minutes later, I was back home.

The next morning, I phoned Maria on my cell phone, hoping that she wasn't busy at that moment, and fortunately, she answered her phone.

"*Bongiorno, cara mia,*" I said in my best Italian accent.

"*Bongiorno,* Jeff, *come va?*"

"*Va bene!*" I answered. "I feel wonderful just to hear your voice! Maria, how would you like to go to my parents' for tea tomorrow afternoon after we come off the beach? I know it's short notice, but have you made any plans for the evening?"

"Oh, Jeff, wow, that would be nice. I would be delighted for both of us to come, and as Carmen will look after Giovanni, I am yours for the evening as well! See you later at two."

About twelve-thirty, I left my home and decided to go to my parents' home. I knew they would have returned from the temple, as the Sabbath service was usually finished by a quarter to twelve.

I had had a quick snack for lunch, and had packed a towel and drinks, which I'd put into the trunk of my car, and off I went.

The sun was shining and the weather forecast was good, and life was great! "Hi there!" I said as I went down the stairs to where they would be.

"Good Shabbes," they called out.

"How was today in the temple?"

"There was a barmitzvah this morning, which was nice, and a Kiddush after the service, but we didn't stop for it."

"I can't stay too long, as I'm due to meet Maria and Giovanni at two. Maria said she'd be delighted to come to tea, so I will see you both about four thirty." I kissed them goodbye and made my way out of the house. I then got into my car and made my way to where Maria lived.

CHAPTER 20

It was just before two as I entered the beach entrance, and I saw them sitting under a large parasol. Next to her was Giovanni, making castles in the sand. I walked down the pathway and then onto the sand where they were sitting.

"Ciao," I said.

Maria looked up, and I bent down and kissed her on her cheek. I then said 'hi' to Giovanni. He smiled at me, as if he knew who I was, and this pleased me a great deal.

I found a beach bed to sit on next to Maria and put my bag down, which contained my towel and drinks. Then I spread my towel over the bed and proceeded to take my clothes off and leave my swim shorts on that I had on underneath.

I sat down and stared at Maria in her black bikini, looking as alluring as that time in Stresa. She really was so beautiful, and I was glad our paths had led to each other. We took turns to put sun cream on each other before we basked in the now hot sunshine without a care in the world.

At around four, we decided it was time to leave, so we folded everything away and walked up the beach to the promenade.

As my car was not fixed with a child car seat, we carefully strapped Giovanni inside the seat belt, put the buggy in the trunk, and Maria got into the back next to him, while I got into the front.

"I want to return to my home first to have a quick change and freshen up. It won't take longer than ten minutes."

"Okay, Maria, let's go!"

Twenty minutes later, we were on our way with Giovanni also now changed, and Maria in a top and skirt, driving up the highway to my parents' beach house.

When we arrived, I rang the bell, pressed the code, and the front door opened.

"We're here!" I called out, and I led Maria, who was holding Giovanni carefully. We walked down the spiral staircase and into one of the living rooms, where my mother and father were.

When we entered the room, they were already standing and first my mother, then my father hugged both of us, kissed us, and of course, 'our son.'

"Sit down and make yourselves at home. How was the beach?" my mother said without giving us a chance to speak.

"What a handsome little boy! How old is he?" my father interrupted. He looked down at Giovanni, who was still holding Maria's hand, and smiled. "What is your name?"

"My name is Giovanni," Giovanni replied to Maria's surprise, as Giovanni was usually shy with strangers. He had obviously picked up some English since going to a local nursery.

"And how old are you?" my father asked.

Giovanni had trouble understanding this, so Maria said, "He will be four on June 18th, in a few months' time."

"Let me hold him," Sandy asked. "He looks just like Jeff did when...when Jeff was that age!"

This innocent remark was made without my mother realizing how true her statement was, and I wondered whether we should tell them both or not?

Maria lifted Giovanni up and handed him to my mother. Giovanni, who was not used to strangers holding him, just smiled and put both his arms on my mother's shoulder, as if he'd known them for all his short life. Maria and I were amazed!

"Look at this, David," my mother said, "he's taken to me like we're old friends!"

I looked at Maria, and she winked at me.

My father said, "Well, that's a good start, hon. Let's hope he feels the same about me! And by the way, Maria, call us David and Sandy, we don't stand on ceremony here!"

Ten minutes later, my mother announced that tea would be ready, and we all got up and made our way onto the terrace where we sat down round a large table.

"Sandy, let me give you a hand," Maria said.

"Oh, thank you, Maria, come with me."

The two ladies went inside to bring plates, bagels, and what had been prepared in advance before the Sabbath commenced.

While I was alone with my father, he turned to me. "Jeff, you definitely take after me. Your taste in women never disappoints me. Maria is lovely, and what a wonderful child!"

At that moment, the two ladies appeared with two trays carrying plates, cups, saucers, bagels, and different fillings.

My mother placed everything on the table and went back inside for the tea and coffee.

"Where exactly do you come from, Maria? Do you have a family here, and how long are you here for?"

Three questions in quick succession!

The questions went on and on, and Maria answered all of them. My parents never asked any leading questions, like who Giovanni's father was, so it was all very friendly.

"Sandy and David, as you know, I nursed Jeff back to full health while he was in the hospital. We became wonderful friends, and I even took him to see my family in Stresa."

"Maria has a wonderful family," I said, "very similar to ours in the way they are all close and loving. You would have to get to know them really well, and, Mom, you would have loved Maria's mother."

My father listened intently but had a puzzled look on his face, which Maria noticed.

"Oh, by the way, you may have noticed the 'Star of David' around my neck." Maria hesitated and then continued, "This was a present that Jeff bought me when he said goodbye to me. I must confess that I am not Jewish, but in my spare time, I have studied your religion and feel I know a lot about your customs."

This took me by surprise. Maria had not mentioned this before, but it certainly made me feel good.

My parents were also taken aback, but they didn't show that they were bothered.

Maria, who was seated next to me, at that moment of confession, rested her hand on mine. My parents noticed this and looked at each other and smiled.

Was it at all remotely possible that they would accept Maria? Only time would tell.

Then the conversation shifted to my side of the family, and my mother proceeded to tell Maria about my sister, brothers, and all their wives and children. Time passed very quickly, and the conversion flowed.

I looked at my watch and couldn't believe it was six-thirty and time to go. We gathered our things and made our way to the elevator. It had been a lovely afternoon, and I think it could not have gone any better.

"Thank you for a lovely time and for making me feel so welcome," Maria said to my parents.

"You're welcome any time. Let us know when you're free on a Friday night, and then you and Giovanni must come for a 'Shabbes' meal."

"Oh, that would be nice, Sandy. I'd also like to learn some Jewish cooking!"

"We'll make a date, let Jeff know. God Bless," my mother said and hugged Maria.

"See you both soon!" my father said as he looked down, smiling at Giovanni, who was yawning. He then gave Maria a hug.

"Good Shabbes!" Maria said to our surprise.

Then, with Giovanni, she stepped into the elevator, followed by me, and we pressed the button for the top floor.

CHAPTER 21

"You certainly made an impression! And when did you start studying Judaism?"

"When I was in Italy during my pregnancy, Father Giancarlo managed to get hold of some books for me. One was called '*A Guide to Jewish Knowledge*,' which was very helpful. All the festivals, the Jewish calendar, and why they are celebrated!"

"Then you probably know more than me and can teach me a few things!" I chuckled.

I was now at Maria's home and was about to leave for mine.

"I'll pick you up in a couple of hours, and we'll go for a drive to Laguna Hills, where there is a cozy restaurant."

"Okay, Jeff, *ci vediamo*, and thank you for this lovely afternoon!"

Later, after a shower and a change of clothes, I was ready to call for Maria.

It was eight thirty. I rang Maria's bell, and after a minute, she opened the door.

"*Ciao*," I said, and bent down to kiss her on the cheek.

"I'm going now," she called out to Carmen, and with that, she stepped out and closed the door behind her.

We drove into the hills and eventually came to this dimly lit building with a car park at the side of it. Outside the front door in neon lights was a sign that said 'Valentino's.'

"A table for two, please," I said as the waiter approached us and duly guided us to a table by the window overlooking a small floodlit lake.

As usual, Maria looked like an angel, this time in pink and white, with a carnation fixed to her hair on the side.

The waiter took our order of two well-done steaks with salad and a bottle of red wine, and then we looked at each other as if there was no one else in what was a crowded restaurant.

"Well, Maria, what a day this is turning out to be!"

"I'm so glad your parents liked me. We'll have to tell them who Giovanni really is. I wonder how they will take it?"

"There's only one way to find out, but I'm sure it will be a wonderful surprise for them."

We ate our meal, and soon it was ten o'clock. I paid the check, and we left for Maria's home.

"Maria, will you stay with me tonight?" I had to ask her that as it just felt like the thing to do.

"Jeff, I did have a little work to catch up on, and I have nothing to wear. Moreover, Giovanni will expect me in the morning."

"We could stop off at your place. You could leave a message with Carmen, and you could just take some clothes for tomorrow."

Maria looked at me and smiled. "I don't usually do these things like this on a second date—what would everybody think?"

I could see she was joking now, and I grabbed her, kissed her passionately on the lips, and said, "Never mind what people would think. One day, we will tell the whole world how we feel about each other. Also, you don't need any underwear either; in Laguna Beach, it's the done thing to sleep totally nude on the second date! Furthermore, ever since the last time I saw you without clothes, I can honestly say that you are perfection, and you've no reason to be modest in front of me!"

"You're a good talker, Jeff. I'd like to hear you say that in Italian!"

"There's only one thing I'd like to say this moment in Italian, and that is, '*Ti adoro*,' and perhaps, '*Voglio fare l'amore con te!*'"

Maria smiled and said, "I would like to make love to you, spoken like a true Italian, Jeff. *Che sara, sara!*"

We arrived at Maria's, where she wrote a note and carefully placed it on the kitchen table. She then went to the bathroom, collected a few essentials, and came out of her front door, locking it behind her.

Not long after, I opened my own front door, let Maria step inside, and then proceeded to chase Maria around the room.

She was quick and darted around the table, chairs, and sofa before making for the patio doors, which, stupidly, I had left slightly open by mistake.

She closed them while I stood there with my hands on my hips, watching her as she slowly danced, taking first her pink top off and turning her back to me. She suddenly turned around and undid the zip of her white skirt, which slowly slid down past her hips to the floor. She then picked it up and covered her front with one hand while undoing her bra with the other. Then she held out her bra and let it drop.

Swaying side to side, she maneuvered her hips, and very slowly and sexily, lowered her panties until she stood there naked in front of me.

I stood there transfixed, wondering just what she would do next. She slowly walked towards me and lifted my 'T' shirt up over my head and threw it onto the nearby table. Then she put her hands on my pants' belt and undid the catch.

I had an enormous erection by now, so I bent down, lifted her up, and put her over my shoulder and walked to my bedroom, where I put her on the bed, switched on the bedside lamp, slid my shoes off, and lay beside her.

I took my underpants off and slowly moved my body on top of her, kissing her face, her neck, her lips, then her breasts, gradually working my way down to more intimate places.

The passion grew stronger, and I could hear her moaning with pleasure. I then pulled her on top of me so she was facing me, and I entered her, watching her every movement as she rose up and down, until we reached a breathtaking crescendo.

"Maria, Maria, I never want to let you go again! I don't care anymore what people might think, we were meant to be together!"

Maria was silent for a minute, and then she spoke, "Jeff, *mi amore*, I would like nothing better than to spend my life with you. There has never been anyone else that I have even felt like this about or shared such intimacy with. Maybe, we should talk to your parents?"

After this rush of passion, I should have taken precautions, and it was silly of me. I just didn't think...

We lay in each other's arms for quite a while and then drifted off to sleep. The next time I looked at the bedside clock, it was seven-thirty.

I rose from my bed, and at that moment, Maria stirred. "Good morning, Jeff, and how are you feeling this bright morning?"

"Oh, good morning. I feel like I have won the lottery!"

The sun was shining through the large windows now. Maria got out of bed, too, and we both made our way to the bathroom to have a shower.

"Ladies first," I said.

But Maria replied, "Why don't we shower together?"

So, we did, soaping each other from head to foot. It was difficult to concentrate on what we were supposed to do.

Then we got out, and I reached for two clean towels, one for Maria and one for me, dried ourselves, put some clothes on, and made for the kitchen.

I found two mugs, made the coffee and toast, and we brought our breakfast back into my living room, where we sat.

Two very happy people, who just wanted to be together forever!

CHAPTER 22

I took Maria home around nine-thirty, and as we arrived at her front door, who should be standing there but Carmen holding Giovanni's hand?

"Good morning, signora, and how are you this lovely morning? "

Carmen, being Mexican, was picking up not only the English language but also Italian due to Giovanni speaking Italian to his mother.

Although there were a number of similar words and phrases, she sometimes became confused. Luckily, her English was reasonable from what she had learnt at school, so she and Maria were able to converse mainly in that.

"It's a wonderful morning, Carmen. To me, there has never been a morning like it! I have some news for you. I am going to take a few days' leave, and we will be moving into Jeff's beach home. It's very spacious and is on two floors, and there is plenty of room for the three of us. I hope to get off on Wednesday, so be prepared to get your things together."

Back at Jeff's parents, Sandy and David had just had their breakfast on the terrace.

She had been searching through some old photos of when their children were young, and she was looking for one specific photo of the time when Jeff was a child. She couldn't find it.

"I can't find that photo, David, you know, the one at Gary's birthday party?"

"Why do you want it, hon? It could be anywhere."

"Oh, I don't know, it's just that Giovanni reminds me so much of when Jeff was his age. I just had to satisfy myself and find it. Jeff had the same colored hair as a child, and he had your coloring. Moreover, you had black hair."

David replied, "Maria also has dark coloration, and her hair is also black, so this is quite normal for him to have her coloring."

"But, David, I'm not imagining it, but I think Giovanni even looks a little like our son."

"Sandy, you're making too much out of this, so just forget about the child!"

Sandy got up and put the large box containing the many photos back where she had found them and cleared up the breakfast things.

David then said, "Why don't you call Jeff and see if he would like to come over to lunch with Maria and Giovanni?"

Sandy wondered if they were pushing it a bit, but still went to the phone and dialled Jeff's number.

"Hi, honey, it's Mom. How are you doing? Did you have a good time last night? Would you three like to come over for lunch? Well, call me back then. We can sit and relax or do anything you'd like."

Sandy put down the phone and told David that Jeff wasn't sure what his arrangements were.

Jeff really wasn't sure how to approach his parents at some point about Giovanni, but he was sure that he and Maria had to be together, no matter what.

CHAPTER 23

Jeff called Maria and asked what she was doing. Her told her that his mother had asked them over for lunch if she hadn't made any arrangements.

"It's very nice of them, Jeff, but I have to do some sorting out with clothes, etc., if I am coming over to your home. It's Carmen's day off, so I have to keep an eye on Giovanni as well. Also, I have some reading to do for work."

"Okay, Maria, let's leave it then. I want to go for a run to keep my fitness up, and maybe later, call on my parents. I'll phone you later. I miss you already!"

"I miss you, too, Jeff. Soon, we will be together!"

Jeff phoned his mother to say they wouldn't be coming but that he might pop in later. He then locked up and started to jog at a slow pace along the coast path.

After half an hour, he turned around and made his way back, feeling refreshed and so very happy the way things were working out for his family.

After a quick shower, Jeff dressed and sat down and read the Saturday newspapers that had been delivered and then fell asleep.

He was dreaming. It was his wedding day to Maria in a secluded part of the beach. Chairs in rows of ten, covered in white satin, with large bows on the back and divided by an aisle down the middle. At the end, facing the ocean was a 'chuppah,' a Jewish canopy, decorated with white lilies and red roses.

Seated behind him on one side were his mother and father, his family and his parents' friends, and seated on the other side of the aisle were Maria's family, who had flown from Italy to be there. The rest were all Jeff's friends and some work colleagues of his and Maria's.

A Mexican Mariachi band of five, all dressed in white, with white sombreros, and holding guitars, was standing nearby, ready to play. The bride, Maria, held her brother's arm, ready to make her way to the Chuppah, where the groom, Jeff, was waiting!

Jeff turned, opened his eyes, and realized that it was all a dream. He had been asleep for a couple of hours, and it was gone one o'clock. The dream had been so real, could it one day be reality?

He went to the kitchen and made himself a light snack, washed it down with some black coffee, and picked up the phone to call Maria.

After four rings, Maria answered. "Hi, gorgeous! How's it going?"

"Hi Jeff, okay, I guess, lots of clothes still to pack and moving things around."

"Can I help? I don't want you to pull a muscle or something. I could come over and take a few cases, plus Giovanni and I could play something or watch TV?"

Jeff was so hard to resist for even a few hours, so Maria replied, "Okay, see you soon!"

Twenty minutes later, Jeff rang Maria's bell.

When she opened it, Jeff entered and hugged and kissed Maria. She then held his hand and took him through to where Giovanni was watching the television.

Jeff walked up to him, bent down, and gave him a big hug. "*Ciao*, Giovanni, how are you today?"

"Hi, Jeff," he said, "I watch the television," not knowing the correct way to say it.

Maria looked at the two of them, so pleased that Giovanni had taken a liking to the man who was his father. She then asked Jeff to come into her bedroom to move the full cases.

The room was fairly large, beautifully decorated in pink and white bed sheets and pillow cases, with white walls and beige carpets.

There were two cases ready to be taken, so Jeff got hold of one of them and took it to the front door, and then he returned for the second one.

Maria said, "I hope you can get everything into your home."

"Don't worry, I can shift my clothes around, and I have closets in all three bedrooms, most of which are almost empty. Carmen will have a room to herself, and she will have her own bathroom like us! The only bedroom that I use, anyway, is mine."

"It sounds great, Jeff, come into the kitchen now, as I think you deserve a cold drink"

Jeff wondered if he should tell Maria of his dream. Could this really be happening to him?

Then he suddenly remembered that the photo of when he was Giovanni's age was in an old photo album at the top of his closet. His mother had mentioned this photo to him when they had spoken earlier, and that she couldn't find it.

"I have an idea, Maria. Why don't we take Giovanni out just for a short break to have some tea and drive down to Dana Point by the harbor?"

"That would be nice. Just give me time to put some other clothes on."

"Great, I just want to call my mother, and when you're both ready, we'll go."

Maria left the bedroom while Jeff telephoned his parents.

"Hi Mom, I'm at Maria's now. I've asked her to move into my home with Giovanni and Carmen, so she's been packing her belongings."

"Okay, son, send our best wishes. We'll speak tomorrow."

He walked into Maria's living room, where Giovanni was watching a Disney program, sat down, and waited for Maria.

Ten minutes later, she appeared, spoke to Giovanni in Italian, switched off the TV, and then they made their way to Jeff's car outside.

Maria got into the back with Giovanni. Jeff started the engine, and they were off.

Some fifteen minutes later, they arrived at Dana Point's car park, got out of the car, and made their way to the café, which thankfully wasn't busy. They found a table for the three of them.

The waitress saw them and came over with the menus. Both knew what they wanted. Maria ordered a waffle and ice cream for Giovanni with some orange squash, and for the two of them, two tea cakes, and a pot of English tea, with some milk.

Jeff thought, *She's already ordering things for me that I like. In fact, I could get used to this idea!*

The food soon came. It was all very tasty, and Giovanni finished all that he was given.

Jeff and Maria talked between eating about her family, and how they were coping without her mother.

Maria said that she spoke to them nearly every day and that everything was fine. Their vineyards had done exceptionally well this year, and things were looking good.

Soon, it was time to go, so Jeff settled with the waitress. They then left the café, got into the car, and before long, they were back at Maria's.

They loaded some of her baggage into the trunk of Jeff's car, and he returned to his home.

After taking the cases into the spare room, Jeff returned to Maria's, where they sat and watched a movie on the television.

When it was Giovanni's bedtime, Maria bathed him, and she let Jeff help her.

The feelings that they had were something too wonderful to describe, and the love he had for his little boy was also something that he had never imagined.

After they had put Giovanni to bed, they kissed him goodnight and left a small lamp on in his room until he was asleep.

In the living room, Jeff sat and held Maria's hands and said, *"Cara mia,* we will at some point tell my parents that Giovanni is my son, and you will have to tell your family."

"Jeff, you're right. But when I became pregnant, I had to tell my mother and family—how could I not?—and even Father Giancarlo."

"So they know then? How did they take it?"

"Well, they guessed that you were the father, but, as they were very fond of you, I told them how we had felt about each other, and, although they were disappointed that I was pregnant, they were happy it was you.

"Now, when I speak to them, they always ask after you, and I have told them that you know now that you are Giovanni's father. So, I think that we will only have to tell your parents."

"How about tomorrow then?" Jeff asked. "Let's invite them over for tea tomorrow."

CHAPTER 24

Jeff returned home later, and before he left for Maria's, he called his parents.

They agreed to come over at three, and he mentioned that he and Maria had something to tell them.

At two o'clock, the next day, on a sunny afternoon, Maria came over with Giovanni.

As usual, she looked lovely with a pink 'T' shirt and white pants, while Giovanni was wearing his favorite soccer shirt with *'LAGUNA LIONS'* printed on the front and 'Giovanni' printed on the back.

Maria had been to the local deli and had bought some food, which they both put onto plates, setting the table. Then, right on three, the doorbell rang, and Maria went to answer it.

"Hi, come in, lovely to see you again!"

She hugged David and Sandy.

On hearing their voices, Giovanni came running to the front door to see who it was. When he saw them, his face lit up, and they bent down, and he shook their hands like he was a 'grown up.'

Then they made their way to the living room, while Giovani went to play with some toys in his bedroom.

As Jeff was sitting next to his mother, he held her hand and said, "Mom and Dad, Maria and Giovanni are moving in with me this weekend. We are very much in love, but there is something else we have to tell you." Jeff got up and went to the side board, where he opened the drawer and took out the photo of himself that Sandy had been looking for. He then returned, sat down, and handed it to her.

"Mom, is this the photo that you've been searching for?"

She took it and replied, "Yes, Jeff, it is!"

"Mom, Giovanni is my son!!!"

There was a silence for thirty seconds, while Sandy studied the photo.

"Oh, darling Jeff," she said, with tears now, beginning to flow down her face, "I could see a likeness to you from the first day I saw Giovanni."

"Mom and Dad, you have another grandson!"

Sandy and then David got up and hugged Maria and Jeff, and the four of them were filled with tears of happiness.

Jeff then said, "Giovanni doesn't know yet that I'm his father as we think that he's too young to take it in, but Maria's family know." Jeff could feel the happiness and jubilation in the room.

"Oh, Jeff, your dad and I are happy for you both! And believe me, Giovanni, Maria, and yourself, will be treated the same as all our family. You will never want for anything, I can assure you!"

Maria then called Giovanni as it was time for tea. He came into the living room, and even so young, he could sense that something had happened, as everyone looked so happy.

Then, they all made their way to the dining room, where the food was on the table, wrapped up in cling film.

Giovanni sat in the chair between Maria and Sandy, and he helped himself to an egg bagel and potato chips, quite grown up for a child so young.

Maria went to the kitchen and brought in the tea, coffee, and pastries, and everyone tucked into the tasty food.

It was difficult in a way to discuss the future, but Maria wanted to know about how Jeff's parents had met and where they came from.

Sandy then spoke, "We came from Brooklyn in New York originally. Our parents came here from Russia to escape the pogroms, and David and I knew each other from childhood. Also, we always knew that one day, we would get married. David studied law at Harvard, while I wanted to be a teacher. We got engaged when we were eighteen, and when David finally qualified and started earning good money, we found a small apartment where we lived, and then we got married.

"Then the opportunity came for David to join a prestigious law firm in California. The money was twice as much as he was earning, and a partnership was David's aim. So, we flew out to L.A., met everyone, and found somewhere to rent. It was a town called Villa Park, not too far from Disneyland and a short ride on the Freeway to Santa Ana, where the law firm had one of their offices. It looked ideal. Far away from the cold winters of New York, though we would miss many of our family and friends.

"We hoped that one day, we would fly our parents out, and we'd find them a place to live. They were all getting on a little, and the warm weather would also be good for them. David progressed and was doing really well, and then I became pregnant with Gary.

"I had managed to get a teaching job at the local school, but when David started earning big bucks, I gave it up to look after our child. David eventually became a partner, but he felt that he was doing so well that he wanted to start on his own, and so, he left, found a suitable premises in L.A., and formed 'David Gold Lawyers Inc.'

"That was a long time ago. Our sons, Gary and Michael, are now partners in the firm, and we have many branches, but Lana, our daughter, will qualify soon to be a doctor."

Maria listened intently and was happy to know something about Jeff's family, which would now be hers. Who knows that one day, she and Jeff might even be married, which might be a little complicated, as Jeff was Jewish and she, Roman Catholic. For the time being, though, she would enjoy one of the happiest moments of her life, and '*Che sarà, sarà!*'

When tea was over, everybody went out via Jeff's bedroom's patio doors onto the terrace and relaxed on the seats under the large awning, as the sun was still quite strong.

Giovanni had also come and was happy to sit on Sandy's lap while she was attempting to teach him some more English phrases, which his little brain took in.

Jeff thought that with Giovanni going to a school that spoke English and his folks and himself speaking that language, Giovanni would soon be bilingual, like his mother. Moreover, with Carmen speaking Spanish, he would end up being trilingual. Wow!

The afternoon was perfect, and their timing couldn't have been better.

A little after five, David and Sandy decided to leave, so they got up, kissed Maria and Jeff, and hugged their new grandson Giovanni, thanked Jeff and Maria for a marvelous and memorable afternoon, made their way to the front door, and went home.

"Wait till we tell everyone, David! I knew it, I had a strong feeling as Giovanni's likeness to Jeff as a child was uncanny. Also, he has Jeff's black hair, is tall for his age...oh, David!"

Tears formed in Sandy's eyes again.

CHAPTER 25

Carmen returned at seven, and we decided to tell her the news that I was Giovanni's father.

She was also pleased for us and said, "*¡Felicitades a todos!*"—*Congratulations to all of you!*

Both Maria and I had to be up early the next day as it was Monday again, so, as much as I wanted to stay, I left for my home. She would be busy until Wednesday, when she took off another three days' leave, to finish packing and make the move to my place.

Everything seemed perfect now!

On Saturday morning, the removal van I had hired turned up at Maria's, and a sturdy-built man and his colleague loaded the final items of furniture from her place. Then Maria, Giovanni, and I got in my car, and Carmen got in hers, and we led the van driver to where I lived.

By the evening, it was nearly all unpacked.

The clothes were neatly put in drawers and hung in respective closets, and thanks to the help of the removal men, Carmen and Giovanni's beds were now in their respective bedrooms.

In Carmen's room, there was also a television, so Maria and I could have some privacy if we wanted, and all that was left was for Maria to return her keys to the owner of her home in due course.

By nine o'clock, we were all exhausted. We said goodnight to Carmen, hugged Giovanni, as he lay in his bed in his new surroundings, and he took it all in his stride.

"Good night, *buona notte, buenas noches,*" we both said, in English, Italian, and Spanish.

"Good night," Giovanni and Carmen replied together in English.

Then Maria and I returned to our bedroom, showered, undressed, and got into bed. I turned off the light, and Maria fell into my arms, and I held her tight. "*Ti amo, te quiero,*"—*I love you*—she said.

"Three languages, Maria—you speak Spanish as well?"

"No, Giovanni told me that 'I love you' in Spanish is '*te quiero!*'"

Jeff answered, "Our son is going to be so clever. All-American/Italian sportsman. Maybe a lawyer or doctor? Does he sing well? There have been so many American Italian well-known singers here, so maybe we might have another one in the future?"

"God willing, Jeff. Now, *ti adoro*,"—*I adore you*—"let's just go to sleep."

We could faintly hear through the gap in our patio doors the sound of the waves on the Pacific Ocean, and soon, we were both asleep.

This weekend had been another memorable time in the lives of our families.

CHAPTER 26

The days and weeks went by. Maria, Giovanni, and Carmen settled into their new home. Maria and Giovanni met my sister, brothers, and their families, and Maria became close to my mother and Lana, which was great. They went out together, shopped together, and it was like a real close family.

Giovanni loved the attention he was getting, and his teachers at his school said how well he was doing, especially his ability to learn English, with, of course, an American accent.

Then June 18th came, which was Giovanni's fourth birthday. Maria and I had invited his little school friends over for afternoon tea, with snacks that the kids would enjoy. The day after, we were invited over to my parents, who were going to put on a party, which included his new cousins, Bradley and Darren, Gary's sons, and Jo and Rachel, Michael's two daughters, who were a little older than Giovanni.

Our love grew stronger every day. Then, just before Giovanni's birthday, after we had returned from dinner in Laguna Hills, we were sitting on the sofa when I got up, went to our bedroom, returned, and got down on one knee in front of Maria.

"Maria, will you marry me?" I asked.

"Oh, yes, yes, I will!" Maria replied, now about to cry with such emotion.

I then placed the diamond ring on her finger and kissed her.

"But Jeff, how can we be married in your Synagogue or Temple, as you call it? You're Jewish and I'm Roman Catholic?"

"Darling Maria, my dad has a good friend who is a federal judge, and he is able to perform wedding ceremonies. Other than that, you could convert to the Reform Jewish religion, but you would have to study for a year or more about our customs, dietary laws, etc. I have spoken to him, and he can't visualize any problems, and he would marry us. In time, if you wanted to, you could have lessons and study about the Jewish faith and maybe convert, but, darling, there's no rush or pressure."

"And what about my family?" Maria replied. "How could they all come?"

"Let's take one step at a time. I'm sure my parents would help."

"Jeff, as you are well aware, I have been reading Jewish books that Father Giancarlo bought for me, and if you and your parents help me, I might, in time, join the Reform—but, as you have said, *one step at a time!*

"I was born a Catholic and raised a Catholic, and, although I have let my faith 'slip' and haven't been to church for some time, it might be better just to be wed in a civil ceremony. To convert might also be upsetting to my family. It's as if you were to convert to Catholicism, and knowing how religious your parents are, how do you think they would feel?"

Maria was right. My parents would be more than upset, and it would break their hearts.

I hugged Maria and said, "I should phone them and tell them the good news!"

She agreed, so I dialed their number.

"Hi, Mom, how are you? I have some news for you. I proposed to Maria, and she said 'yes'!"

"*Muzzal Tov, Muzzal Tov!*" My mother called my dad to tell him. "We'll have to talk about it. Tomorrow's Friday, and the three of you are coming to us for a Shabbes dinner, and we can discuss it then. Oh, Jeff, I so hoped this would happen. See you all about seven! God Bless."

I'm sure my mother would have put down the phone, so elated and excited, as if she had won the state lottery! To me, it was like a wonderful dream come true, and maybe the dream I had that night might even happen as well.

At a quarter to seven the following evening, we were all ready to leave. Maria collected the flowers she had bought to take with her. We then locked up and got into my car, with Giovanni now seated in a child seat that I had bought.

Soon, we were there. After I had pressed the bell and put in the code, I called out, "We're here!"

We proceeded to make our way down the winding stairs to where my parents stood at the bottom, waiting for us with open arms.

"Good Shabbes! Good Shabbes!" they both said together, and we kissed each other.

My mother scooped up Giovanni into her arms, and we made our way to their living room, where we made ourselves comfortable.

I then told my father that I had contacted his friend, William Taylor, who said that he could marry Maria and me, and also, at a later stage, about Maria converting to the Reform religion.

My father thought for a minute and said, "Well, son, I know that you are not 'frum' like your mom and I, but you're my son, and whatever you decide, if it makes you happy, then your mom and I will be happy for you."

Soon, it was time to eat, as the Sabbath time had arrived. We all went into the dining room and stood behind our seats, while my mother lit the Sabbath candles and said the usual Hebrew blessing over them. Then, my dad recited more blessings, and we had a sip of wine and sat down.

Giovanni sat between Maria and my mother on a large cushion on the chair to give him some height, and I sat on the other side next to my dad. Like me, he wore a small 'yamulka' on his head, which was normal in an Orthodox family.

Giovanni had wanted one as well when he saw both my dad and I had our heads covered, and we found him a small one, which we placed on his head, although with his thick curly hair, it was difficult to see.

Then Maria and my mother went into the kitchen where the chicken and vegetables were in China bowls, ready for consumption, and the chicken soup was simmering in a large tureen.

Then, on a trolley, the soup and soup dishes were brought in, and one by one, my mother served the soup, with a special small bowl for Giovanni.

It was delicious and contained 'lockshen' or vermicelli, a traditional pasta to have with the chicken soup. Giovanni finished the lot!

Known in Jewish circles as 'Jewish penicillin,' there was nothing like homemade chicken soup!

When we finished the soup, the ladies brought in three large plates and one small one, with the roast chicken and vegetables, which were like nectar to my mouth, and once again, Giovanni just had a very small portion. Then, this was followed by some fruit salad and non-milk kosher ice cream.

Once we had finished our meal, my dad took out a small prayer book and recited the '*Grace After Meals*,' and soon it was over.

When all the crockery was put into the dishwasher, we all went back to the living room where we spoke about the future.

"Have you thought about a date yet?" my mother inquired.

Maria replied, "No, not yet, but probably next year, which would give us time to get organized and plan it. I'd have to invite my family also, but it would number at least twenty, and I'm not sure if they could afford to come all this way; besides, they have the winery to look after."

"Well," said my dad, "you know my friend, Gerry Davis; he owns a private jet, and if I asked him nicely, maybe he would be able to help."

Maria and I were feeling a little awkward now, as it was a little too much to take in. We both knew that my father and Gerry were exceedingly wealthy people, but to accept all this was a little too much to expect or take for granted.

I realized that my dear parents were so very happy for us, and since money was no object, they wanted to help us, but I needed to discuss this with Maria on our own. So, I said, "Let's leave it for now, Dad—one thing at a time. We will have to leave soon, as I can see Giovanni is yawning, and it's past his bedtime."

"That's okay, Jeff. I just got carried away a little. This is all too exciting, and another 'simcha' to look forward to in the Gold family!"

With that, we got up to go.

"Thank you for a lovely evening and such a memorable occasion," Maria said, and with that, we hugged our hosts.

Giovanni, who was now falling asleep, was lifted up by his new grandfather, and we made our way to the elevator, where we said goodnight.

It was an evening to remember!

CHAPTER 27

Everything now seemed just as Jeff and Maria had hoped for. Maria was now living with Giovanni and Carmen in Jeff's home, and life couldn't be any better.

Then one evening, Maria felt unwell and was decidedly sick. This went on for a week, and then she missed her period.

While at the hospital, she decided to see a close doctor friend in the maternity ward, and after taking a urine test, just as she thought, she discovered she was *pregnant*.

Maria sat there and thought of the time she forgot to take the pill. When her duty for the day had finished, she drove home, still wondering how she really felt, and whether it was the wrong time to have a child with her job coming along so well?

When she arrived home, although it was difficult, she had to tell Jeff, as they kept no secrets from each other. As a further thought, the fact that she was Catholic, abortion was frowned upon.

Jeff, who usually finished at four and was home as usual before her, was in the patio area on his laptop.

"Hi, darling," Maria said as she rested her hands on his broad shoulders. "How was your day?"

"Okay, honey, I've just arranged a soccer game against a local league youth side on Saturday afternoon, and I'm just deciding what my team will be."

"That's great, Jeff, but if you can give me five minutes, I have something I have to tell you."

Jeff saw a worried look on Maria's face and asked her to sit down next to him.

"I missed my period and haven't felt too well for about a week. Today, at the hospital, I saw a colleague, and she confirmed what I thought—*that I am pregnant.*"

Jeff's face lit up with joy, but he saw Maria's face again and realized that something was wrong.

"Jeff, I know how happy you must feel, and I know it's not that we have any money problems, but I'm just about to be promoted to a higher position. Quite honestly, I'm thrilled about it, plus the extra money, and I really don't want to turn it down!

"Having a baby would mean I'd eventually have to give up work. I can't expect Carmen to do more than she does now, so I really don't know what I should do?"

Jeff looked at Maria earnestly and realized that she was not ready for another child yet. "Look, honey, I'll agree to whatever you decide to do, but let's just leave it for a while. Rushing in and making the wrong decision is never the right thing to do, anyway. But, for the moment, I think we should keep this to ourselves, okay?"

"Okay, Jeff," she replied, and with that, a smile returned to Maria's face. She got up, reached for him, and he rose from his chair, and they hugged each other.

Maria then walked through to the living room, where Giovanni was engrossed with Carmen in more English phrases.

"*Ciao*, Giovanni, hi Carmen; how's it going?" Maria bent down and kissed Giovanni on the cheek.

"Signora Maria, Giovanni is doing so well. His little brain seems to absorb most phrases I teach him. Plus the fact that he has to speak English at his school, I think that soon, he will understand and speak English as good as I!"

Giovanni said to Maria in Italian that the children at school now call him '*Gio*,' and Maria smiled.

She replied in Italian and told him that that is what is known as a 'pet' name, but to her and Jeff, he would always be known as Giovanni.

With that, Maria left them both to continue and went to the bedroom.

Sometimes, she would 'Skype' her family on her laptop first thing in the morning when she woke up, as it would be three in the afternoon there.

It was never a convenient time, and she had missed it that morning as she had slept a little later, and of course, they would be working.

Skype, which had come into existence in 2003, was an amazing invention, and Giovanni couldn't get over it. Speaking to his uncles, aunts, and cousins like they were in the next room was a miracle, and Maria had to agree with him.

So, Maria decided to wait until 10.30 that evening, when they would be getting up. She then made for the kitchen and made an evening meal. But Carmen, being so efficient, had sorted out the pasta and tomato sauce, ready to cook, and had even laid the kitchen table where they usually ate, so it was a question of just cooking it.

Thirty minutes later, the four of them were busy enjoying the penne pasta with a glass of red wine for the three of them and some squash for Giovanni.

It was such a happy home, and Giovanni was so contented with everything.

At seven o'clock, he said goodnight to Maria and Jeff, as they stood on each side of his bed and bent down to kiss him.

Carmen, who was like a second mother to him and was standing just behind the other two, then came forward and also kissed him, and the three adults left his bedroom.

Maria thought that Carmen, who had a boyfriend, might one day leave them, and who knows, get married—*then what would she do?* Carmen might want to start her own family, and if that happened, Maria would seriously have to think about giving up work.

CHAPTER 28

July went by, and the good weather continued into August, but Maria was still suffering.

Then, it was more or less decided for her when Carmen wanted to speak to her one Saturday afternoon. Giovanni was at a friend's house, and Carmen's boyfriend was on his way to pick Carmen up. Maria was just resting on the sofa when Carmen came up to her and sat down. "Signora Maria, I have been with you ever since you came here from Italy when Giovanni was a baby. You are like my second family, and I couldn't wish to work anywhere else but here with you, Mr. Jeff, and Giovanni.

"Pablo and I have known each other since childhood. When my family moved from Mexico City to San Diego, he followed me and found a job there. As you know, he works in Los Angeles as a mechanic, and he proposed to me last week, and I accepted. Our families are very similar to your family in Italy. We've always been close, and at last they live in San Diego Old Town, which isn't too far from here, and we visit them whenever we can."

Maria was listening intently and realized what was going to happen. "So, Carmen, you want to give in your notice?"

"Signora, Pablo and I want to be married in San Diego in December, and there is a small apartment we could rent. Pablo has a chance to work in a garage there, which is owned by his cousin, and his parents run a children's nursery and would welcome me to work there."

"Looks like this is all working out for you, and Carmen, you deserve it! So, Carmen, exactly when did you want to leave?"

"It's now August 2nd. I'd like to leave the beginning of September, if it's at all possible?"

Maria got up and embraced Carmen. "Carmen, from the beginning, you have always been included in my family, we all love you, but you have to do what is best for you, and all I can say is '*Felicitades*,' congratulations on your engagement, and I wish you and Pablo lots of good luck and good health in your future lives together. We will always be friends, and hopefully, we will still see each other when you're married. I know that Giovanni will miss you terribly, and will still want to see you constantly!"

And so it happened. At the beginning of September, after a small farewell party given by David and Sandy, Carmen said her goodbyes to people who were like family to her and left with Pablo for San Diego.

Maria had decided to have the baby, and, as she was now four months pregnant, she had gone to see her boss at the hospital the moment that Carmen had given Maria her notice.

"Doctor Grant, I think it's time that I have to leave. My nanny, Carmen, has left, and Giovanni needs me now full time, and I will be expecting a baby, as you know, in February. I have loved working here, but with a baby on the way, it's not possible for me to carry on."

"My dear Maria, you have been a great asset to this hospital, and it will be difficult to find a replacement as good as you, but I wish you all that you wish yourself!"

And with that, Maria got up and left the doctor's office.

After a farewell party in October at the hospital, in which she was given many gifts, Maria left.

On the home front, the Jewish New Year of Rosh Hashanah and the fast of Yom Kippur had just ended, and the Gold family had attended their synagogue, and Jeff also went with his parents.

Then there was the festival of Sukkot, which was an agricultural festival of thanksgiving, and a commemoration of the forty years during which the Children of Israel wandered through the desert after leaving slavery in Egypt.

A 'sukkah' was built in David and Sandy's garden, which was a temporary hut or booth, topped with branches and decorated with harvest items, and the festival lasted for eight days.

Jeff didn't go with his parents to the Temple until the last day, as he couldn't take the time off work, but now that Maria was not working any more, he was pleased she was spending time at home, and resting every afternoon.

Jeff and Maria had told David and Sandy about the pregnancy by this time, as it was now showing, and once again, they were ecstatic with the wonderful news of yet another grandchild.

On the weekends, Jeff decided to decorate Carmen's old room for the nursery and buy a cot and furniture, and soon, it was all taking shape.

CHAPTER 29

Christmas came and went. Maria put up a small Christmas tree for Giovanni and covered it with tinsel and lights, which Giovanni loved. But it was also the Jewish festival of Chanukah, which was also a happy time and during which presents were also given. So, Jeff bought a box of candles and took out the 'menorah,' a special candelabra, from a cabinet, and Maria helped him celebrate the Jewish festival.

It commemorates when the Jewish people fought the Greeks and the miracle of the oil that lasted in the Temple for eight days.

The 'menorah,' which can hold eight candles, is lit each night, and on the first night, one candle plus another that lights the first candle is lit; on the second night, two candles, and so on—each night for eight nights.

Songs are sung, and it is a joyous time, just like Christmas.

New Year's Eve, 2011, was celebrated with families, and on February 11th, 2012, Maria gave birth to a beautiful baby daughter with dark brown eyes and black hair. It was an easy birth, and after three days, Maria came home with Jeff and baby Sophia, which was Maria's mother's name.

The happy couple had decorated the nursery in pink, and it looked like a picture. There was a white cot in the corner with a chest of drawers to match, and so many soft, cuddly toys and baby clothes, plus money, all given as presents.

Giovanni was also thrilled to have a little sister and didn't stop telling all his friends all about her at school. Jeff hired a nurse who came three times a week to help Maria, who was very pleased with the extra help. David and Sandy, of course, seemed to pop in every day, but they also took out Giovanni to relieve Maria of the work.

The wedding of the year was arranged for June, which was only four months away, and Jeff was elated when he discovered that his dream had come true, and they were to be married on the beach, and Judge William Taylor, David's friend, would officiate.

Gerry Davis agreed, for a reasonable price, to have his plane, which could hold twenty-four persons plus luggage, fly to Milan to collect Maria's family, and David agreed to pay for their return flight by one of the national airways, a few days after the wedding.

He had also reserved rooms for all of them at the New Kings Hotel, where they would stay, as the reception was there, and the staff at the winery in Italy would take care of things while everyone was away.

Time flew by, and soon it was June. The women shopped for dresses, Jeff's brothers bought navy tuxedos, and Maria found a wedding dress that was perfect for her.

The bridesmaids, Lana, and Lucy, Maria's best friend, had identical pink dresses, which were bought by Maria, and four-year-old Giovanni had a small tux especially made for him.

In Italy, Maria's brothers had also bought suits to match Jeff's brothers, so everybody was happy.

Then, on a gloriously sunny day on June 21ˢᵗ, everything was set.

At 4 p.m. on Sunset Beach, a canopy with red and white roses fixed around it was set up near the shore, and white satin-covered chairs in rows of ten were placed facing the canopy.

There was an aisle down the middle, separating the chairs, and Jeff's family, friends, and many prominent people that David and Sandy had invited sat on one side.

On the other side sat Maria's family, friends, and ex-colleagues from the hospital.

Maria didn't know it, but Doctor Rossi from the hospital in Milan and Father Giancarlo had also been invited and were also sitting there, and it would be a wonderful surprise for her when she eventually saw them.

Another guest was Samuel Casey, Jeff's old buddy, who was now living in New York with his partner, and Jeff hadn't seen him since Jeff's stay in the hospital; they had flown out the day before to be there.

Jeff was standing silently in his navy tuxedo in front of the canopy.

David and Sandy were seated in the front row with Giovanni in between them, and then Michael, Gary, and their wives.

Suddenly, the music sounded. The mariachi band started to play '*Can't Help Falling in Love*,' by *Elvis*, as they walked down the aisle, and with their white outfits and sombreros trimmed with gold, it could have been the setting for a movie.

Two were playing trumpets, two with guitars, and one playing a violin, and they eventually stopped to the left of the canopy.

Then, a white limousine arrived at the top of the beach, the chauffeur got out and went to the door to open it, and Lucio, Maria's brother, got out, and then he held Maria's hand to help her out.

Then slowly, in time to the music, Maria, escorted by her brother, walked down the aisle, passing the guests and finally stopping where Jeff was standing. Lucio took a seat with his family as Maria stood beside Jeff.

Jeff turned to face Maria, his 'princess.' He couldn't believe what he was seeing.

Maria was wearing a white organza dress, making it ideal for Maria's form and suitable for the warm weather. Cut in layers to add fullness, the scene was the sheer epitome of a romantic garden or beach celebration.

Maria, now smiling at her groom, was also holding a bunch of white lilies and gardenias, looking like an absolute picture!

Jeff almost cried with happiness. Flashes of cameras were going off as photos were being taken of the happy couple, and the professional photographer stood facing the couple, filming the event.

"Hi," she said, with an enormous smile on her face.

"Hi," he replied, trying to hold back tears of joy.

Judge Taylor stood there in front of them, and then there was an enormous surprise for them both. From out of the guests appeared Father Giancarlo, who made his way under the canopy and stood next to Judge Taylor. Maria and Jeff couldn't believe that their friend had come all that way to see them!

After the judge had read out the formalities and Maria and Jeff had read out to each other their vows, Father Giancarlo waited patiently.

Then, as Maria and Jeff exchanged rings, Father Giancarlo blessed them both in Italian and in English with, "May the Lord bless you and protect you. May the Lord make his face to shine on you and be gracious unto you. May the Lord turn his face towards you and give you peace."

And with that, Judge Taylor announced, "I now pronounce you husband and wife, and Jeff, you may kiss your bride!"

Jeff clasped Maria, looked into her beautiful eyes, and kissed her!

Everyone applauded loudly. Father Giancarlo embraced them both, and Jeff and Maria turned, and with the mariachi band starting to play again, they walked slowly down the aisle, where their limo—all draped in white ribbons—waited to take them to the New Kings Hotel, where the reception, dinner, and ball would take place.

Half an hour later, family and friends were walking into the reception, greeting Jeff and Maria, and helping themselves to canapes and champagne.

Little Giovanni was talking to his Italian family, while Lucio's wife, Carla, was looking after baby Sophia, in her 'carry cot,' now four months old.

At five thirty, the master of ceremonies announced very loudly that dinner was served, and the families and guests made their way to the banqueting hall to find their allotted seats.

The room looked amazing, decorated with flowers and balloons on each table, and with each chair—just like on the beach—covered in white satin with large bows at the back.

The top table was made up of Jeff, Maria, David, Sandy, Maria's oldest brother, Lucio, his wife, and Father Giancarlo. Some ten tables were in front of them, along with a long children's table, for Giovanni and his cousins and friends.

When everyone was seated, Father Giancarlo got up and said a short *Grace Before Meals*—careful not to use any religious words, as the majority of the guests were Jewish, and it would not have been appropriate.

Then David arose and made his 'welcome' speech. "My Dear Maria, Jeff, Sandy, Father Giancarlo, family, and friends. What a day! What a momentous occasion in the lives of our two families, the Golds and the Carlottis! Welcome to the wedding of Jeff and Maria! Sandy and I have watched Jeff grow into a fine young man. From the moment he was born with his thick curly black hair, we knew that one day he would find the girl of his dreams, although it's taken him longer than Sandy and I expected!

"He always had a mind of his own, and, much to our shock, joined the army to fight for his country. And by fate, or maybe the Almighty arranged it, when he was badly wounded, he was taken to a hospital in Milan and cared for by the finest staff one could wish for! And, there he DID meet the girl of his dreams, Maria, and what a beauty!

"In the time Sandy and I have gotten to know her, we can see exactly why Jeff fell in love with her. Her charm, her warmth, her care, her loyalty to Jeff, and her family in Italy, and on top of that, as I have previously mentioned, she is a really beautiful young lady! It's great that her close family is here for the wedding, and I pray that we will always have a wonderful friendship, even though they live six thousand miles away.

"May I say that it's also marvelous to see Father Giancarlo and Doctor Rossi here, and I'd like to thank Father for his kind words and blessings, and to Doctor Rossi for the care he gave Jeff in Milan. Moreover, had it not been for Doctor Rossi, who was happy for Maria to take Jeff to meet her family more than once, this relationship may never have happened.

"Although we are of two different religions, we both worship the same God, and when I see the way Jeff looks into Maria's eyes, I realize that there are no boundaries when it comes to matters of the heart! And what about Giovanni? Another grandson for Sandy and me, and baby Sophia, a beautiful granddaughter, just like her mother! I pray that Jeff, Maria, and their children will be blessed with lots of good health and happiness in their future lives. I'd better end now, as I'm really so full of emotion. May I just finish by saying may you all have a wonderful time, may you eat, drink, and be merry, and may we always meet on happy occasions!"

With that, David sat down to rapturous applause. Then the food was served. Tomato or chicken soup, followed by roast chicken or fish, with different vegetables to accompany the courses. When that was finished, a lemon sorbet followed, and then to round it off, fruit salad and kosher milk-free ice cream. There was plenty of champagne and cold drinks, and while they ate, Ray Archer and his band played in the background.

Then, the master of ceremonies announced the different toasts, one to the President of America, given by Michael; everyone stood up and sang the National Anthem, and then one to the President of the State of Israel, given by Lana and then the band played 'The Hatikvah,' the Israeli Anthem, and those who knew the words joined in.

After this, it was the turn of the best man, Gary, who said most of the things his father said about Jeff and Maria, plus a few anecdotes about the past that made everyone laugh.

Then it was Jeff to reply. He stood up and said, "My Darling Maria, Mom and Dad, the Carlotti family, my family, and friends. This is the happiest day of my life, and over the last couple of years, I've had a few extremely happy moments! I was going to make a long speech, but my father has '*stolen my thunder!*' So, I will just say my thanks to someone up there that when I got badly wounded and ended up in the hospital in Milan, I met my Maria!

"I will never forget that moment when I opened my eyes in that hospital bed in the middle of the night, and I did not know where I was or what had happened to me. Then this young nurse came towards me, and I saw a most beautiful vision! I remember it like it was yesterday! I thought that she looked like a young Jean Simmons or Elizabeth Taylor. I was transfixed by her beauty, and when I asked her name, and she said Maria, I thought of that musical, '*West Side Story*,' and the Puerto Rican girl Maria, and the song with the words, '*the most beautiful word I have ever heard!*'

"It was definitely love at first sight! Every time I saw her, I fell more in love with her. When she took me to

Stresa by the Lakes to meet her wonderful family, I knew that there was something that she must have felt about me! And then later, after I had returned to California, and had gone to Fashion Island to buy my mother a birthday present, by chance, fate, or by God's intervention, who should I see in one of the restaurants but Maria and a child?! I believe that it was meant to be!

"And so, my friends, here we are, celebrating the happiest day of our lives! Here I am by the side of the most beautiful woman I have ever seen! Thank you very much for all your wonderful gifts and kind wishes, and have a great evening!" And with that, Jeff sat down, like his father earlier, to thunderous applause.

Then there were shouts, "We want Maria; we want Maria!"

Maria smiled, and, unprepared for a speech, stood up. First of all, she spoke in Italian to her family, as she was sure that they had not understood most of the speeches.

She spoke then in English about her close family, her dear parents, who were no longer there but maybe there in spirit, how they had brought her up, and how she went into nursing rather than the Church—but it was obviously the right decision, as, she wouldn't have met Jeff otherwise!

She then called for Giovanni, and he left where he was sitting and walked to the top table to stand by his mother on one side and his father on the other. Everyone cheered, and Giovanni waved back to them.

Maria continued, "If I hadn't met Jeff..." She looked down at Giovanni, and the guests understood what Maria meant, but little four-year-old Giovanni still didn't know that Jeff was his father.

It would now be time to tell him.

"Sandy and David," Maria turned to Jeff's parents, "thank you for all that you've done for me and for welcoming me into the Gold family and for supporting me! I couldn't wish for better in-laws! And finally, to Jeff, from that first moment that we met, I think I also fell in love with you! God bless you all!"

And with that, she bent down and kissed Giovanni, who then returned to his seat. She sat and hugged Jeff, once again, to non-stop applause.

With the speeches over, it was time to open the ball.

CHAPTER 30

The band had now changed for a while, as Jeff and Maria had also hired a Latin American band, who was known throughout the Americas and was going to play for a while.

It was called the *Santiago Martinez Band*, and the moment the speeches were finished, Jeff and Maria walked to the center of the ballroom, and the band began to play the well-known song 'Besame Mucho' in a rumba rhythm.

During Jeff and Maria's time together, they had taken up Latin American dancing lessons, so they danced the rumba like two professionals to the applause of everyone. Soon, their families and friends joined them, and the party was in full swing! Giovanni danced with Maria and his family, and although it was past his bedtime, he was wide awake and enjoying every minute.

Then, after a while, the band changed, and Ray Archer returned for the rest of the evening.

The time flew by. Coffee and cakes were served at ten, while the band and singers had a short break, and then, after more dancing, the last dance was played at half past midnight.

The band played both National Anthems again, and then Maria and Jeff stood by the entrance to the room, so that everyone could say goodbye to them one by one.

Finally, no one was left except for Maria, Jeff, Giovanni, David, and Sandy. Baby Sophia was upstairs in an adjoining room next to the bridal suite, with the part-time nurse, who had been caring for her since she was born and had come to the wedding earlier.

Carmen and Pablo, who had also been at the wedding, were almost the last to leave, hugging Maria, Jeff, Giovanni, David, and Sandy, telling them what a wonderful day they had had, and hoping that the newlyweds would come to their wedding later that year.

Father Giancarlo and Doctor Rossi had left after the refreshments, as they had an early flight back to Milan; they had embraced the happy couple, who promised to return to Milan and visit them one day.

Finally, David and Sandy said their good nights and went to their room upstairs. Jeff and Maria were left to retire with Giovanni to their bridal suite, and after undressing him, they settled him into the adjoining room.

CHAPTER 31

In the bridal suite, Jeff and Maria sat Giovanni on the bed with them.

Maria smiled at her son, gently brushing a hand through his hair. "Five years old already," she said. "Your birthday was just a few days ago, and we promised you that after the wedding, we'd have a proper party for you once we're back from our honeymoon."

She paused, and her expressions softened. "But tonight, before bed, Jeff and I want to tell you something really important."

Maria put her arms around Giovanni and said, "Giovanni, you've grown to love Jeff as if he were your 'papa,' and he loves you as if you were his son. My darling, Jeff *is* your real papa. When you are a little older, we will tell you more, but it's very late now, and I know you are very tired."

Giovanni, who was so intelligent and mature for his age, hugged Maria, and then Jeff, who was also seated on the bed.

"*Capisco*, Mama, I understand, Mama," he said. Then he reached over and hugged his father.

For a few minutes, the three of them just hugged and kissed each other, and everything couldn't have been better.

Maria then helped Giovanni undress, and he kissed his father goodnight, while Maria opened the adjoining door, and quietly helped her son into his bed near where the nurse was sleeping next to Sophia's cot and kissed him goodnight. "*Bonna Notte*," she said.

She then returned to her room, got undressed, showered, and got into the four-poster bed that had been covered with red rose petals.

Jeff did the same.

They just lay there, looking into each other's eyes, so happy that they were almost lost for words.

Jeff then turned and faced Maria, telling her, "Maria, we met when I woke up in that hospital bed. I didn't know where I was or what happened to me, but then I saw YOU. The most beautiful creature came to my bedside, as you know, I thought you were a cross between a young Elizabeth Taylor and Jean Simmons. And it was you who saved my life in many different ways. You shared my lonely days, you comforted me when I was feeling low, you made me want to become the man I am now, you shared your family with me, and eventually shared your body with me!

"A Roman Catholic girl and a Jewish boy who fell in love against all obstacles that might have stopped this happening. It was as they say, '*Forbidden Fruit*,' but we made it work. '*Ti amero sempre!*' I will love you forever!"

Maria, kissed Jeff, reached for the lamp, switched it off, and then they made love....

ABOUT THE AUTHOR

At 81 years young, Peter Collins resides in North West London, where he enjoys the company of his son, daughter, and two beautiful granddaughters. As a widower, Peter's family means the world to him.

Having faced life's challenges, including the untimely loss of his wife, Peter drew upon his personal experiences to write this novel. His story is one of resilience, offering a mix of happiness, humor, and poignant moments that will undoubtedly touch the hearts of many.

Peter's novel is a testament to the strength of the human spirit and the universal experiences that connect us all. It's a story filled with heart—one not to be missed.